Swedish Fairy Tales

Herman Hofberg

Swedish Fairy Tales

Legends of Trolls,
Elves, Fairies & Giants

Herman Hofberg

Swedish Fairy Tales:
Legends of Trolls, Elves, Fairies, and Giants

Originally published as *Swedish Fairy Tales*, Homewood Publishing Company, Chicago, 1902. Layout and design © 2009 by Joanne Asala.

Author: Herman Hofberg
Translator: W. H. Myers
Editor and Designer: Joanne Asala

ISBN 10: 1-880954-09-5
ISBN 13: 978-1-880954-09-6

Published by:

Kalevala Books
An Imprint of
Compass Rose Technologies, Inc.
PO Box 409095
Chicago, IL 60640
www.CompassRose.com

Front cover image: Illustration for "The Boy Who Never Was Afraid" by Alfred Smedberg in the anthology *Among Pixies and Trolls*, 1912. Back cover: (Top) Illustration for "The Changeling" by Helena Nyblom in the anthology *Among Pixies and Trolls,* 1913; (bottom) illustration for "The Boy and the Trolls" by Walter Stenström in the anthology *Among Pixies and Trolls*, 1915.

Contents

Author's Preface

It is probably known to most readers that there is a distinction between Tradition and Saga. Tradition has, or at least seems to have, to do with facts, usually designating some particular spot or region where the incident is said to have taken place, often even giving the names of actors, while the Saga is entirely free in its scope, equally as regards incident, and the time and place of its happening. Not infrequently the traditions of a people are founded upon actual historical occurrences, which, often repeated in the naive manner of the peasantry, become, finally, folk-lore. A great many are, however, drawn from ancient myths, which, in time, become clad in historical garb, and are located in some particular place.

We already possess various collections of traditions drawn from the rich treasury of our peasantry, but up to the present there has been no attempt at a formulated compilation of Swedish folk-lore. As I now put into the hands of the public such a collection, I ought to state that I have thought it better to select the most typical of our traditions than to gather everything that I might in this line, much of which has already been written, and which would require a many times larger volume, and occasion a repetition of the same matter when occurring, as many do, in different localities. Instead, I have accompanied each tale with a historical and ethnographical note in which I have so stated if the tradition is found in different places.

The illustrations are the product of several among our best artists. Without doubt, the book has thereby been added to greatly, not only in outer adornment, but even in national and intrinsic value.

Herman Hofberg

Translator's Preface

An interest in the Swedish people, their language, their literature and history; the important part the traditions of a people play in their history, character and domestic life, and that the traditions of the world play in its history and that of mankind, and that I would, if possible, add to the growing interest in that far-away, beautiful country, and that generous, hospitable people, have been the incentives to the labor involved in this translation; a labor not unmixed with pleasure, and not a little of that pleasure coming from the encouragement of my Swedish acquaintances.

No embellishment and not more than a faithful reproduction of the author's ideas have been attempted, and I shall be happy, indeed, if I have done so excellent a writer as Mr. Hofberg, approximate justice in this regard.

I have taken the liberty to leave out a number of the author's notes as unimportant, and not likely to interest the general reader, also to follow the stories with their notes instead of grouping them in the back of the book as in the original.

The Sure Shot

It is not alone in Bohemia's mountainous regions that the romantic characters are found which form the basis of Weber's immortal fictions. Similar traditions are current in many lands, especially in ours, one of which we will now relate.

In the artless fancy of the peasantry the means of acquiring the power of unerring aim are many, the most usual by compact with the Fairies or Wood Nymphs. While the compact lasts the possessor, sitting at his hut door, needs only to wish, and the game of his choice springs into view, and within range of his never-failing gun. Such a compact, however, invariably ends in the destruction of the hunter.

Many years ago there was a watchman up in the Göinge regions, a wild fellow, who, one evening, while drinking with his neighbors, more tipsy and more talkative as the hour grew late, boasted loudly of his marksmanship, and offered to wager that, with his trusty gun, he could give them such an exhibition of skill as they had never before seen.

"There goes, as I speak," said he, "a roe on Halland's Mountains."

His companions laughed at him, not believing that he could know what was transpiring at a distance of several miles, which was the least that lay between them and the spot indicated.

"I will wager you that I need go no farther than the door to shoot him for you," persevered the watchman in defiant tones.

"Nonsense!" said the others.

"Come, will you wager something worth the while? Say two cans of ale."

"Done! Two cans of ale, it shall be." And the company betook themselves to the yard in front of the hut.

It was a frosty autumn evening. The wind chased the clouds over the sky, and the half moon cast fitful reflections through the breaks over the neighborhood. In a few minutes a something was seen moving rapidly along the edge of a thicket on the farther side of a little glade. The watchman threw his gun carelessly to his shoulder and fired. A derisive laugh was echo to the report. No mortal, thought they, in such uncertain light and at such a distance, could shoot a deer in flight.

The watchman, certain of his game, hastened across the glade, followed by his companions, to whom the event meant, at least, two cans of ale.

It would not be easy to picture the surprise of the doubters, when, upon arriving at the thicket, they discovered, lying upon the ground, bathed in foam and his tongue hanging from his mouth, a magnificent stag, pierced through the heart by the deadly bullet, his life blood fast coloring his bed of autumn leaves a brighter hue.

What unseen power has brought this poor animal from Halland's Mountains in a bare half hour? Such were the thoughts of the watchman's companions as they retired in silence to the hut.

The watchman received his two cans of ale, but no one seemed inclined to join him in disposing of them. They now understood with what sort of a man they were having to do. It was evident to them that the watchman was in league with the Evil One himself, and they henceforth guarded themselves carefully against companionship with him after dark.

Herman Hofberg

Stompe Pilt

At a little distance from Baal Mountain, in the parish of Filkes-tad, in Willand's Härad, lies a hill where, formerly, lived a giant named Stompe Pilt.

It happened one day, that a Goatherd came that way, driving his goats before him, up the hill.

"Who comes there?" demanded the Giant, rushing out of the hill, with a large flint stone in his fist, when he discovered the Goatherd.

"It is I, if you will know," responded the Herder, continuing his way up the hill with his flock.

"If you come up here I will squeeze you into fragments as I do this stone," shrieked the Giant, and crushed the stone between his fingers into fine sand.

"Then I will squeeze water out of you as I do out of this stone," replied the Herder, taking a new-made cheese from his bag and squeezing it so that the whey ran between his fingers to the ground.

"Are you not afraid?" asked the Giant.

"Not of you," replied the Herder.

"Then let us fight," continued Stompe Pilt.

"All right," responded the Goatherd, "but let us first taunt each other so that we will become right angry, for taunting will beget anger and anger will give us cause to fight."

"Very well, and I will begin," said the Giant.

"Go ahead, and I will follow you," said the Herder.

"You shall become a crooked nose hobgoblin," cried the Giant.

"You shall become a flying devil," retorted the Herder, and from his bow shot a sharp arrow into the body of the Giant.

"What is that?" inquired the Giant, endeavoring to pull the arrow from his flesh.

"That is a taunt," replied the Herder.

"Why has it feathers?" asked the Giant.

"In order that it may fly straight and rapidly," answered the Herder.

"Why does it stick so fast?" asked the Giant.

"Because it has taken root in your body," was the answer.

"Have you more of such?" inquired the Giant.

"There, you have another," said the Herder, and shot another arrow into the Giant's body.

"Aj! Aj!" shrieked Stompe Pilt; "are you not angry enough to fight?"

"No. I have not yet taunted you enough," replied the Herder, setting an arrow to his bowstring.

"Drive your goats where you will. I can't endure your taunting, much less your blows," shrieked Stompe Pilt, and sprang into the hill again.

Thus the Herder was saved by means of his bravery and ingenuity.

The Giant Finn*

In the days long gone by there lived in Helgonabacken—the Hills of Helgona—near Lund, a family of giants who one day heard, with great anxiety and consternation, that a holy man had come into the country, from Saxony, to build a church to the White Christ.

While Laurentius, such was the holy man's name, was selecting his site and laying out the plans for the temple, there stood at his side, one day, none other than Finn, the giant of Helgonabacken, who thus addressed him: "Truly the White Christ is a God worthy of such a temple, and I will build it for you, if, when it is finished, you will tell me what my name is; but, mark well my condition, oh, wise man, if you cannot tell me, you must give to my little ones the two small torches—the sun and the moon—that travel yonder over heaven's expanse."

Now, it is so ordered in the giant world that it is of vital importance the name of the giant should be kept from mankind. Should it be revealed the giant must die, and man is freed from all obligations that may have been imposed upon him by compact with the giant. Laurentius could not reasonably promise so much, but anxious to have the church built, he offered, instead, his eyes, trusting to fortune to discover to him the giant's name before the completion of the church. The giant, satisfied with the bargain, entered at once upon his work, and with wonderful rapidity the church grew upward. Soon there remained nothing more to complete it than to set one stone on the tower.

The day preceding that on which it was expected this last stone

---

* Similar legends are connected with a number of our churches, as the cathedral of Trondhjem, where the Troll is called "Skalle." Also with Eskellsätter's church in the department of Näs in Vermland, where the giant architect is called Kinn, who fell from the tower when the priest Eskil called, "Kinn, set the point right!" Again, with a church in Norrland, where the Troll is called "Wind and Weather," and concerning whom the legend relates "that just as the giant was putting up the cross, St. Olof said, "Wind and Weather you have set the spire awry." Of the church at Kallundborg in Själland, whose designer, Ebern Snare, it is said, entered into a contract much the same as that made with the Giant Finn by the holy Laurentius.

would be put in place Laurentius stood on Helgonabacken in deep melancholy. It seemed inevitable that he must lose his eyes, and that he was now taking his last look at the light of heaven and all that had made the world and life so attractive to him. Next day all would be darkness and sorrow. During these gloomy reflections he heard the cry of a child from within the hill, and the voice of the giant mother endeavoring to quiet it with a song, in which he clearly distinguished the words: "Silent, silent, little son of mine, morning will bring your father Finn, with either moon and sun or the priest Laurentius' eyes."

Beside himself with joy, Laurentius hastened to the church. "Come down, Finn!" he cried, "the stone that now remains we ourselves can set—come down, Finn, we no longer need your help!"

Foaming with rage, the Giant rushed from the tower to the ground, and laying hold of one of the pillars tried to pull the church down. At this instant his wife with her child joined him. She, too, grasped a pillar and would help her husband in the work of destruction, but just as the building was tottering to the point of falling, they were both turned to stones, and there they lie today, each embracing a pillar.

Herman Hofberg

The Lord of Rosendal

In the beginning of the Sixteenth Century there lived in Skåne a nobleman, Andres Bille, Lord of Rosendal, who was very severe toward his dependents, and it was not unusual that a disobedient servant was put in chains, and even into the castle dungeons.

One day Bille's intended made a visit to Rosendal. Upon entering the courtyard almost the first object that attracted her attention was a peasant tethered like a horse. She inquiring as to the cause of such treatment, Bille informed her that the servant had come late to work, and was now suffering only well merited punishment. The young woman begged Bille to set the man at liberty, but this he refused to do, and told her, emphatically, that she must not interpose in his affairs.

"When the intended wife," said the young lady, as she returned to her carriage, "is refused a boon so small, what will be the fate of the wife?" and thereupon she commanded her coachman to drive her home at once, and resolved to come no more to Rosendal.

People predicted that such a heartless man could not possibly be at rest in his grave, and true to the prediction, Bille, after his death and burial, came every night, in spirit, to Rosendal. Halting his white team in the courtyard, with stealthy steps he would make his way to his former bed-chamber where he would spend the night until cock-crow. If the bed had been prepared all was quiet in the chamber, otherwise such a dreadful noise followed that there was no such thing as sleep in the castle. Always, upon going to the room in the morning, the bed clothes were found tossed about and soiled as if a dog had occupied the bed.

When the specter had gone on in this manner for a number of years, the new owner of the estate applied to a pious priest in Hässlunda, Master Steffan, and begged him to put a stop to these troublesome visits. To this end the priest, one day, accompanied by a fellow priest, set out for Kropp's Church, where Bille was buried. On the stroke of 12 o'clock, midnight, the grave opened and the ghost of the dead lord stepped forth. Father Steffan's companion at once took to his heels, but Father Steffan remained and began to read from a book he had with him. During the reading the ghost became larger and larger, but the priest would not be frightened. Finally the apparition interrupted the reading and addressed the priest.

"Is that you, Steffan, the goose thief?"

"It is, indeed, I," replied the priest, "and it is true that in my boyhood I stole a goose, but with the money received for the goose I bought a Bible, and with that Bible I will send you to hell, you evil spirit." Whereupon he struck the specter such a blow on the forehead with the Bible that it sank again into purgatory.

Unfortunately, because of the truth of Bille's accusation and that it came from Bille, the priest's prayers and reading lost much of potency, and he was unable to enforce upon the ghost entire quietude. Nevertheless, so much was accomplished that Bille now comes to Rosendal only once a year.

The Master of Ugerup[*]

In the parish of Köpinge, on the northern bank of a stream which, a short distance below Lake Helga, flows into the river Helga, lies an old mansion, Ugerup or Ugarp, known in early days as the seat of the Ugerup family, famous in the history of Denmark.

In the middle of the Sixteenth Century the estate was owned by Senator Axel Ugerup. On the Näs estate, a few miles distant, dwelt the wealthy Tage Thott, at that time one of the richest men in Skåne.

Herr Arild, Axel Ugerup's son, and Thale, Tage Thott's fair daughter, had, it may be said, grown up together, and even in childhood, had conceived a strong love for each other.

When Arild was yet a young man he was made ambassador to Sweden by the Danish Government, in which capacity he took part in the coronation of Erik XIV. Upon his return to Ugerup he renewed his attentions to his boyhood's love, and without difficulty obtained her consent and that of her parents to a union.

Not long thereafter war broke out between Sweden and Denmark. With anxiety and distress the lovers heard the call to arms.

---

[*] Arild Ugerup, the character in chief of this legend, was born in the year 1528 in the castle of Sölversborg, where his father, Axel Ugerup, was master. When the son had passed through the parochial school of Herrevad, and had attained to the age of manhood, he marched, with others, to guard the old Kristian Tyrann in Kallundsborg castle. Some years later he was sent as Danish ambassador, to be present at the crowning of King Erik XIV, when he was made Knight of the Order of St. Salvador. Later he was sent as envoy to the Russian court, and in 1587 was raised to Lord of Helsingborg, where he died in 1587, and was buried in Ugerup (now Köpinge) church.

Another legend, in which the seeds of the pine tree were sown, comes from Östergötland. A lady of the nobility, living in Sölberga, had a son, who, in the battle of Stångebro, took sides with King Sigismund, and when the battle was lost had to fly the country. The aged mother mourned deeply over her son's absence, and besieged Duke Karl with prayers to allow her misguided son to return home, to make her a visit, at least.

At last he was granted permission to return and visit his mother until, the order read, "The next harvest." Whereupon the mother sowed pine seeds on the fields of Sölberg, which accounts for the uncommonly fine forests of pine even now existing on the estate.

Herman Hofberg

The flower of Danish knighthood hastened to place themselves under the ensign of their country, where even for Arild Ugerup a place was prepared. At leave taking the lovers promised each other eternal fidelity, and Arild was soon in Copenhagen, where he was given a position in the navy.

In the beginning the Danes met with some success, but soon the tables were turned. At Öland Klas Kristenson Horn defeated the united Danish and Leibich flotillas, capturing three ships with their crews and belongings. Among the captured was Arild Ugerup, who was carried, a prisoner, to Stockholm, where three short years before he was an honored visitor and won his knightly spurs.

The friends of Arild entertained little hope that they would ever see him again, and his rivals for the hand of Thale persistently renewed their suits. Tage Thott, who saw his daughter decline the attentions of one lover after another, decided, finally, that this conduct must not continue, and made known to his daughter that she must choose a husband from among the many available and desirable young men seeking her hand. Thale took this announcement very much to heart, but her prayers and tears were without avail. Spring succeeded winter and no Arild came. Meanwhile, the unrelenting father had made a choice and fixed upon a day when the union should take place.

During this time Arild, languishing in his prison, busied his brain in the effort to find some means of escape, but plan after plan was rejected as impracticable, until it occurred to him to make use of his rank and acquaintance with the King. So, not long thereafter, he sent to King Erik a petition, asking permission to go home on parole, for the purpose of solemnizing his wedding, also to be permitted to remain long enough in Ugerup to sow and gather his crops. The King readily granted his petition, since Arild promised, on his knightly honor, to return to his confinement as soon as his harvest was ripe.

He at once hastened to Skåne where he was not long in learning what had transpired during his absence, and that Thale, at her father's bidding, was about to be wedded to another. Continuing his journey to Näs, where his arrival caused both rejoicing and consternation, he presented himself to Tage and demanded Thale to wife, as had been promised him. Knight Tage, however, would not listen to such a thing as a change from his plans, and declared firmly that his daughter should belong to him whom he had selected for her, but Arild made a speedy end to the trouble. By strategy, he carried his bride away in secret to Denmark, where they were shortly afterward married. Tage, outwitted, made the best of the matter and accepted the situation, whereupon Arild and his wife returned to Ugerup.

Arild now had time to think about his promise to the King, and how he might, at the same time, keep it and not be separated from his wife. It would now profit to sow seeds that would not mature soon, so the fields that had heretofore been devoted to corn were planted with the seeds of the pine tree.

When the autumn had passed, and the King thought the harvest must, by this time, have been gathered, he sent Arild a request to come to Stockholm. But Arild convinced the messenger that his seeds had not yet sprouted, much less ripened.

When King Erik was made acquainted with the state of affairs, he could do no less than approve the ingenious method adopted by Arild to obtain his freedom without breaking his word, and allowed the matter to rest.

The product of Arild's pine seeds is now shown in a magnificent forest at Ugerup.

Many other stories are told in Skåne about Arild Ugerup and his wife. Among others, it is related of the former that he was endowed with marvelous strength, and that in the arch of the gateway opening into the estate was a pair of iron hooks, which, when coming home from Helsingborg, Arild was wont to catch hold of, and lift himself and horse together some distance off the ground, after which little exercise he would ride on.

His wife, Thale, was, like her husband, very strong, very good and benevolent, likewise very generous toward her dependents. A story is told of her, that one mid-summer evening, when the servants of the estate were gathered on the green for a dance, she requested her husband to give the people as much food and drink as she could carry at one load, and her request being, of course, granted, she piled up two great heaps of beef, pork and bread, which, with two barrels of ale, one under each arm, she carried out onto the green with ease.

The Ghost of Fjelkinge

During the early half of the Seventeenth Century many of the best estates in Skåne belonged to the family of Barkenow, or more correctly, to the principal representative of the family, Madame Margaretta Barkenow, daughter of the renowned general and governor-general, Count Rutger Von Ascheberg, and wife of Colonel Kjell Kristofer Barkenow.

A widow at twenty-nine, she took upon herself the management of her many estates, in the conduct of which she ever manifested an indomitable, indefatigable energy, and a never-ceasing care for her numerous dependents.

On a journey over her estates, Madame Margaretta came, one

evening, to Fjelkinge's inn, and persisted in sleeping in a room which was called the "ghost's room." A traveler had, a few years before, slept in this room, and as it was supposed had been murdered, at least the man and his effects had disappeared, leaving no trace of what had become of them. After this his ghost appeared in the room nightly, and those who were acquainted with the circumstance, traveled to the next post, in the dark, rather than choose such quarters for the night. Margaretta was, however, not among this number. She possessed greater courage, and without fear chose the chamber for her sleeping room.

After her evening prayers she retired to bed and sleep, leaving the lamp burning. At twelve o'clock she was awakened by the lifting up of two boards in the floor, and from the opening a bloody form appeared, with a cloven head hanging upon its shoulders.

"Noble lady," whispered the apparition, "I beg you prepare, for a murdered man, a resting place in consecrated ground, and speed the murderer to his just punishment."

Pure in heart, therefore not alarmed, Lady Margaretta beckoned the apparition to come nearer, which it did, informing her that it had entreated others, who after the murder had slept in the room, but that none had the courage to comply. Then Lady Margaretta took from her finger a gold ring, laid it in the gaping wound, and bound the apparition's head up with her pocket handerchief. With a glance of unspeakable thankfulness the ghost revealed the name of the murderer and disappeared noiselessly beneath the floor.

The following morning Lady Margaretta instructed the bailiff of the estate to assemble the people at the post house, where she informed them what had happened during the night, and commanded that the planks of the floor be taken up. Here, under the ground, was discovered a half-decomposed corpse, with the countess' ring in the hole in its skull, and her handkerchief bound around its head.

At sight of this, one of those present grew pale and fainted to the ground. Upon being revived he confessed that he had murdered the traveler and robbed him of his goods. He was condemned to death for his crime, and the murdered man received burial in the parish church-yard.

The ring, which is peculiarly formed and set with a large grayish chased stone, remains even now in the keeping of the Barkenow family, and is believed to possess miraculous powers in sickness, against evil spirits and other misfortunes. When one of the family dies it is said that a red, bloodlike spot appears upon the stone.

Herman Hofberg

Ljungby Horn and Pipe*

On the estates of Ljungby there lies a large stone called Maglestone, under which the Trolls, in olden times, were wont to assemble and, with dancing and games, celebrate their Christmas.

One Christmas night Lady Cissela Ulfstand, sitting in her mansion, listening to the merry-making of the Trolls under the stone, and curious to have a better knowledge of these mysterious mountain people, assembled her menservants and promised the best horse in her stables to him who would ride to Maglestone, at Vesper hour, and bring her a full account of the doings there.

One of her swains, a daring young fellow, accepted the offer, and a little later set out on his way. Arriving at the stone, he discovered it lifted from the ground, supported on pillars of gold, and under it the Trolls in the midst of their revelry.

Upon discovering the horseman a young Troll woman, leaving the others, approached him bearing a drinking horn and pipe. These, upon reaching his side, she placed in the young man's hand, with directions to first drink from the horn to the health of the Mountain King, then blow three times on the pipe, at the same

---

* Both of these Troll treasures are now preserved at Ljungby and are willingly shown to curious travelers. The horn is in the form of a half circle and adorned with silver mountings. The pipe is of ivory, made so that it may be blown from either end, and the sound from it is a single piercing note.

When Lady Oellegard Gyllerstierna, who inherited Ljungby, married Cay Lycke, she took the horn and pipe with her to Denmark. The evil that soon befell Lycke was regarded by many as the consequence of Troll curses, which followed him who took the articles from Ljungby. From Lycke the horn came into the possession of Lord Axel Juul, whose widow presented it to the Chancellor, Ove Juul. His son sent it to the Danish minister, Luxdorf. Since 1691 the horn and pipe have remained continuously at Ljungby.

In all quarters of the country similar legends are current, more or less founded upon the Ljungby legend.

As late as the present year (1888) the translator met a gentleman, recently from Sweden, and from the province in which Ljungby is located, who states that the horn is still in the possession of the owners of the Ljungby estate, and that this story concerning it is still current and quite generally believed.

time whispering some words of caution in his ears, whereupon he threw the contents of the horn over his shoulder and set off at the utmost speed, over fields and meadows, toward home. The Trolls followed him closely with great clamor, but he flew before them across the drawbridge, which was at once pulled up, and proceeded to place the horn and pipe in the hands of his mistress.

Outside, across the moat, the Trolls now stood, promising Lady Cissela great happiness and riches if she would return to them their horn and pipe, and declaring that, otherwise, great misfortune and destruction would overtake her and her family, and that it should go especially hard with the young man who had dared to deprive them of the precious articles. True to the predictions, the young man died on the third day thereafter and the horse which he rode fell dead a day later.

During the war of 1645 Field Marshal Gustaf Horn, whose headquarters were at Fjelkinge, having heard this story, and wishing to see the horn and pipe, requested that they be brought to him. The possessor, Axel Gyllerstierna, who then owned Ljungby, forwarded them, accompanied with earnest prayers that they be returned to him as soon as possible. Horn's curiosity was soon satisfied, and he felt no desire to retain them longer in his possession, for while he did he was disturbed every night by unseemly noises about his quarters, which ceased, when, under the escort of a company of cavalry, he sent them back to Ljungby.

Ten years later there took place a still more wonderful circumstance. Henrik Nilsson, the priest at Ljungby, borrowed the strange articles for the purpose of showing them to his brothers-in-law who were then visiting him. During the night the priest's mother-in-law, Lady Anna Conradi, who was one of the family, was awakened by the light of a candle in her room. The bed curtains were drawn back and upon her bed a basket was dropped wherein sat five small children, who in chorus set up a cry:

"O you, who are noted for your kindness, please return to us our horn!"

To her question why they desired it and what value it had to them, they answered:

"For our people's sake."

When she would no longer listen to their pleading they departed, saying they would come again three nights later.

On Thursday night, and the third following their first visit, there was again a light in her room. When Lady Anna drew back the bed curtain she discovered her chamber occupied by a great number of little men, and among them the Troll King himself, approaching her under a canopy of silver cloth upheld on silver poles borne by four servants. His skin was a dark brown and his hair, of which only a tuft was left on his forehead and one by each ear, black and woolly. Softly he neared the bed, holding forth a horn richly adorned with gold chains and massive gold buttons, which he proffered the lady in exchange for the genuine horn. But she was not to be persuaded, and consigned them to God, if they belonged to him, and to the devil, if they were his offspring, whereupon the Trolls quietly and sorrowfully departed.

Soon thereafter it was reported that a peasant's child had been carried off by the Trolls. By means of ringing the church bells it was, however, returned to its mother. The boy related that the Trolls were not pretty, but had large noses and mouths; that the man under Maglestone was called Klausa and his wife Otta. That they sucked the moisture from the food of mankind and so sustained themselves; that they obeyed one king; that they were often at variance with each other; also, that they spoke the language of the country. Lord Chancellor Covet, who published, "A Narrative of Ljungby Horn and Pipe," dated February 11, 1692, says that he knew this boy, who was then twenty-seven years old, also his mother, but admits that both were disposed to superstition and that their understandings were as feeble as their bodies.

The Swan Maiden

A young peasant, in the parish of Mellby, who often amused himself with hunting, saw one day three swans flying toward him, which settled down upon the strand of a sound nearby.

Approaching the place, he was astonished at seeing the three swans divest themselves of their feathery attire, which they threw into the grass, and three maidens of dazzling beauty step forth and spring into the water.

After sporting in the waves awhile they returned to the land, where they resumed their former garb and shape and flew away in the same direction from which they came.

Herman Hofberg

One of them, the youngest and fairest, had, in the meantime, so smitten the young hunter that neither night nor day could he tear his thoughts from the bright image.

His mother, noticing that something was wrong with her son, and that the chase, which had formerly been his favorite pleasure, had lost its attractions, asked him finally the cause of his melancholy, whereupon he related to her what he had seen, and declared that there was no longer any happiness in this life for him if he could not possess the fair swan maiden.

"Nothing is easier," said the mother. "Go at sunset next Thursday evening to the place where you last saw her. When the three swans come give attention to where your chosen one lays her feathery garb, take it and hasten away."

The young man listened to his mother's instructions, and, betaking himself, the following Thursday evening, to a convenient hiding place near the sound, he waited, with impatience, the coming of the swans. The sun was just sinking behind the trees when the young man's ears were greeted by a whizzing in the air, and the three swans settled down upon the beach, as on their former visit.

As soon as they had laid off their swan attire they were again transformed into the most beautiful maidens, and, springing out upon the white sand, they were soon enjoying themselves in the water.

From his hiding place the young hunter had taken careful note of where his enchantress had laid her swan feathers. Stealing softly forth, he took them and returned to his place of concealment in the surrounding foliage.

Soon thereafter two of the swans were heard to fly away, but the third, in search of her clothes, discovered the young man, before whom, believing him responsible for their disappearance, she fell upon her knees and prayed that her swan attire might be returned to her. The hunter was, however, unwilling to yield the beautiful prize, and, casting a cloak around her shoulders, carried her home.

Preparations were soon made for a magnificent wedding,

Swedish Fairy Tales

which took place in due form, and the young couple dwelt lovingly and contentedly together.

One Thursday evening, seven years later, the hunter related to her how he had sought and won his wife. He brought forth and showed her, also, the white swan feathers of her former days. No sooner were they placed in her hands than she was transformed once more into a swan, and instantly took flight through the open window. In breathless astonishment, the man stared wildly after his rapidly vanishing wife, and before a year and a day had passed, he was laid, with his longings and sorrows, in his allotted place in the village church-yard.

Herman Hofberg

The Knight of Ellenholm

Many, many years ago there lived, in Ellenholm Castle, a knight, who, wishing to attend Christmas matins at Morrum's Church, with a long journey before him, and anxious to be present if possible at first matins, set out from the castle, accompanied by his groom, immediately after midnight. Some distance on the way, feeling sleepy, he instructed the groom to ride on while he dismounted and sat down by the roadside, at the foot of a mountain, to take a nap and refresh himself.

He had been sitting only a few minutes when a monster giantess came and bade him follow her into the mountain, which he did, and was conducted to the presence of her giant husband. Here all kinds of tempting viands were set before him, but the Knight, who knew well into what kind of company he had fallen, declined to partake of the food.

Offended at this, the woman drew forth a knife and addressed the Knight:

"Do you recognize this? It is the one with which you chopped me in the thigh when, one time, I was gathering hay for my calves. Father, what do you think we ought to do with him?"

"Let him go," said the Giant. "We can do nothing to him for he invokes the Great Master too much."

"So be it," said the Giantess, "but he shall have something to remember me by." Whereupon she broke the Knight's little finger.

He soon discovered himself in the open air again, and the groom who had returned to search for his master found him in the place where he had left him, but with a little finger broken— a warning to everyone not to sleep on the way to church.

The Trolls in Skurugata[*]

It is generally understood that Trolls, when their territory is encroached upon by mankind, withdraw to some more secluded place. So when Eksjö was built, those that dwelt in that vicinity moved to Skurugata, a defile between two high mountains whose perpendicular sides rise so near to each other as to leave the bottom in continual semi-darkness and gloom.

Here, it may be supposed, they were left in peace and tranquility. Not so, however, for it is related that upon the occasion of the annual meeting of troops at Ränneslätt, a whole battalion of Småland grenadiers repeatedly marched through, with beating drums and blowing horns, and that sometimes they fired a volley from their guns, which so alarmed the Trolls that it is now a question whether any are still remaining there.

In the neighborhood of the same mountain gulch is a very sacred fountain where those living thereabouts in former times are said to have offered sacrifices to their patron saint. Whether this custom is now continued is not known. As intelligence increases this and all other peculiar customs will soon belong entirely to the province of tradition. A few decades ago this was not so; then one could, according to the narrations of old men and women, have had the pleasure of both seeing and talking with the Trolls.

There was once a hunter named Pelle Katt, who, one day, went to Skurugata for the purpose of shooting woodcock, but though it was the mating season, when birds are ordinarily plenty and tame, the hunt was unsuccessful. It was as though ordained. The puffy woodcock and his hens kept out of the way of the murder-

---

* Skurugata is a street-like chasm cut through one of the granite mountains situated in the parish of Eksjö, in width about twenty-five feet, with walls of rock on either side rising precipitously to the height of 130 feet, and in length about a quarter of a Swedish mile—one and one-half English miles. That the fertile fancies of the people have made this wild place the resort of Trolls and other supernatural beings is not surprising. Above the cliff lies a rock called Skuruhatt, by the side of which is an opening into the mountain called Sacristian, where the heathens are said to have made offerings to their gods.

Herman Hofberg

ous shot. Pelle was angry, and suspecting that the Trolls had be-witched his gun, he swore and cursed the Trolls generally, and especially those that lived in Skurugata, whose mouth he was just passing, when a woman stepped out, small in stature and peculiar in feature, bearing a little poodle dog in her arms.

"I bring you greeting from my mistress; she says you are to shoot this dog," said she, approaching Pelle.

"Tie it there to that tree and it shall be done before it can get upon its feet," answered Pelle.

This was done, and the little woman disappeared between the mountains. Pelle raised his gun and sent a charge of shot through the dog's head. But what a sight met his gaze when the smoke had disappeared! There lay his own little child wrapped in a dog's hide.

Pelle Katt's habits were not the best. He was fond of drink, quarrelsome and boisterous, and often in his drunken fits de-clared that he feared neither God nor the devil.

Now, for the first time in his life, he was amazed and crest-fallen.

"O God! What have I now done!" he cried.

His knees smote together and the sweat ran copiously from every pore.

"Here you have your reward," said the Troll woman, who now reappeared and threw a dollar piece to Pelle, so that it fell in his open hand, to which it stuck fast, and hastily picking up the dead child bore it away.

In a rage, Pelle threw the dollar piece after the vanishing fig-ure, at the same time calling out:

"I will take no pay from you for such a deed. Here you have your gift again, you detestable Troll."

A hoarse laugh answered from the mountain.

Pelle went home. The child was absent. His wife cried, but Pelle kept still and went to the ale house. He had no money with which to buy brandy in order to drown his sorrows, but after his old custom he stuck his fingers in his vest pocket to feel if there might not be a penny there. Behold! There was the dollar piece

Trollen i Skurugata

Herman Hofberg

which he had recently cast from him. He dropped it upon the ale house counter and received a drink which truly made him forget his dead child, his wife, himself, heaven, hell and all.

When he became sober the coin was again found in his pocket. He again threw it away, and several times thereafter, but always found it in his pocket when searching it for money. So he continued to drink more and more daily, until, finally, he drank himself into that sleep that knows no waking.

So goes the story of Pelle Katt and the Trolls in Skurugata.

Kettil Runske[*]

On the island of Vising, in Lake Vetter, there lived in olden times two mighty kings, the one in Näsbo and the other in the castle of Borga, at opposite extremities of the island. A controversy arising about the division of land, the King of Näsbo consulted a Troll named Gilbertil, who lived in the parish of Ölmstad, in Östergötland, and engaged him to dig a ditch through the island, thus dividing it into two parts. Gilbertil undertook the work, and began digging at Näs, where a deep pit, even to this day, is pointed out as marking the spot. When the king of Borga became aware of this, he sent an invitation to Kettil Runske, another notorious Troll man who lived in the parish of Habo, in Vestergötland. Kettil Runske accepted the invitation, and at once set out for the island with the returning messengers, to whom his presence on the boat, though he was invisible, was made known because of the boat being borne down into the water to its gunwale. They were also made aware of his departure from them, when they neared the castle,

[*] Commissioned by Governor Lindehkelm and Doctor Urban Hiarne, Bailiff Girs, of Tveta, in the province of Jöenköeping, went to Vising Island in the year 1705, for the purpose of learning whether or no any trace of the Giant's work yet remained.

Arriving at the island he applied to three aged and trustworthy men, from each of whom he received the same narration that has here been presented. Accompanied by these men he went by sea along the eastern coast of the island until he reached a high bluff, situated between the villages of Näs and Stiby, and about a third of a mile south of Visingborg. Here were actually two holes about fifty feet distant from each other. Into these holes three men crept. Policeman Nils Runske into one, and two peasants into the other. After creeping on hands and knees some feet they found it possible to walk upright for about thirty-four feet when the three met, the two tunnels here continuing in a single passage, which they were not able to penetrate beyond a few feet because of the foul air. The passage was six feet high and eight feet wide, but said to have been much larger seventy years earlier. Later Girs was shown a sunken place or bog which extended from the aforementioned bluff inland three-eighths of a mile and terminated at the hole in Kumlaby meadow, where it is supposed Gilbertil is imprisoned. As late as the beginning of the eighteenth century the story was so generally credited that few or none could be found who were not entirely convinced that Gilbertil was still, by some devilish power, alive and laboring to free himself from his imprisonment.

Herman Hofberg

by the sudden rising of the boat as if relieved of a heavy burden. To accomplish his undertaking, Gilbertil intended, apparently, to make an underground canal from shore to shore of the island, and allow the water to complete the excavation, and had already progressed to a point just north of Kumlaby, about half way through the island, when Kettil discovered his whereabouts, and opening the grounds above him commanded Gilbertil to cease digging. Gilbertil met the command with mockery and scorn, whereupon Kettil threw his Troll staff at him. Gilbertil intercepted the missile in the air, but his hands clove to the staff so that he could not free them. In the effort to release himself he endeavored to break it with his feet, but they also stuck to it. In extreme rage he then attempted to tear himself loose with his teeth, which also became fastened. Thus bound, hands, feet and mouth, Kettil threw him into the deep hole which is now to be seen in the meadow of Kumlaby, and which has received the name of Gilbertil's hole.

Dame Soåsan*

In early times there lived in Soåsan, a range of hills not far from the well-known city of Eksjö, a woman Troll who was called Dame Soåsan. She and her forefathers had, for ages, dwelt there, but when the soldiers came and fired their guns—cracked their nuts, as the mountain folk expressed it—on the camp ground of Ränneslätt, the place became intolerable to her and she departed to her sister's, an equally distinguished Troll, who lived in Skuru-

* The inhabitants of Eksjö and thereabouts relate many stories of Trolls and the like, but these are the most complete and characteristic.

Herman Hofberg

gata, which has been mentioned in a preceding story.

Dame Soåsan was very clever and rich, also the possessor of a very bad temper. It was advisable, therefore, not to anger her in any way, for such as were so unfortunate were instantly punished.

A trooper of that time, belonging to the Hussars of Småland, by name Grevendal, serving under Apelarp in Flisby parish, stood one morning on guard in a distant part of the drill grounds, when he saw, wandering toward him along the edge of a wood, a very little old woman, whom he rashly assailed with scoffing and vile epithets, whereupon he received a blow on the ear from some unseen hand, which sent him flying to the top of a tall pine tree near by, where he remained unable to descend until assisted down by his comrades.

Toward those who were careful not to offend her the woman exhibited much kindness and extended many favors. A poor old woman of the human family living near Soåsan, in a little hut, was one time in great distress, her table bare and no one near to help her, with famine already a guest in her hut, menacing her with terrible glare.

Late one evening a knock was heard upon the hut door.

"Come in, in the name of the Lord," answered the old woman, wondering who her visitor might be.

"In that name I cannot enter, but here is work for you from the mistress of the mountain. Spin beautiful yarn, but do not wet the threads with spittle, for then it will become christened and that the madam will not tolerate."

"Where shall I leave the yarn?" asked the trembling woman.

"Go straight forward into the woods, where you will find a smooth green lawn. Lay the yarn there and next day you shall have your pay."

The old woman began at once to spin the flax which she found outside the cottage door, but during the work stood a vessel of water beside her with which to wet the thread.

The yarn was soon finished and she betook herself, with profit and pleasure in prospect, to the wood. As the Troll's servant maid had declared she came to a beautiful glade encircled by high trees.

She there laid down the yarn and hastened to return home, not daring to look behind her. The next day she went again to the spot and found a new bundle of flax, also several silver pieces.

Now followed a period of prosperity for the poor woman. She accumulated money from her work, became rich, but at the same time avaricious, and forgot the prayers, which she had never before neglected, when she retired to rest.

Finally, she did not even trouble herself to keep faith with the Trolls, but spun the yarn according to general custom, wetting the thread with her spittle.

The skeins of yarn were deposited in the usual place, but when she went the next day to get her reward she was unable to find the glade again, and in the end went astray in the woods, from which she did not succeed in finding her way home before a whole day later. Upon arriving home, as was her everyday custom, she brought forth and was about to count over her money, when she found that all the silver pieces had been transformed into small stones.

Want pursued her now with greater severity than ever, for none would help one who was known to have had to do with the infamous Soåsan dame, and the old woman died shortly after in great poverty and distress.

***

A girl who many years ago was a servant in the house of a Senator of Eksjö, named Lind, went one day to find the cattle, which usually grazed in the woods surrounding Soåsan. The animals, for some time back, had not thrived upon the pastures allotted them and were wont to wander far away in search of food, it was supposed, so, at times the girl, notwithstanding the most diligent search, was unable to find them, and when they were found, the cows had already been milked. This day she went plodding sadly along through the dark woods, thinking of the scolding which awaited her at home, when she returned with neither cows nor milk; her mind was also busied with the many stories she had heard about ghosts and Trolls who infested the woods, when she saw two pair of Pigmies, a boy and girl, sitting under the shadow of a large pine tree.

"It is best to be polite when on the Trolls' own ground," thought the girl. Whereupon she addressed the Troll infants in a very friendly manner and invited each to partake of some bread and butter which she had with her in her little bag. The children ate with exceeding greed, a disgusting sight, as they had extremely large mouths into which the bread and butter vanished rapidly. When the girl was about to depart she heard a voice saying, "As you have taken pity on my children, you shall hereafter escape searching after the cows. Go home! They stand at the gate."

From that day the girl no longer had to search for the cows; they came to the gate every night of their own accord, sweet-laden with a rich tribute of the most excellent milk.

The Giant Puke[*]

In the parish of Lofta in the department of North Tjust there lies, near the sea, a mountain called Puke Mountain. From the land side running into the mountain, there is a long fissure terminating in a cave or hall, where formerly lived a Giant called Puke, concerning whom many stories are still quite prevalent among the people.

When the church at Lofta was built the Giant was sorely tormented by the church bells. He suffered great discomfort even from the water courses which gurgled out of the mountain, and in a meadow directly north of Lofta Church, was formed a pond, Kofre Spring, in which holy baptism was sometimes performed.

Puke often declared that he must depart from his mountain because of Kofre Spring and Lofta scolding, meaning the church bells in Lofta.

One Sunday the Giant was more than usually disturbed by the long continued bell ringing, and sent his daughter to the top of the mountain, from which, with her apron strings converted into a sling, she threw an enormous stone at the church tower. But the force was too great, and the stone fell upon the other side of the church, where it lies to this day, as large as a good sized cottage.

Some days later the giant maiden, while wandering over the surrounding country, was attracted by three children at play on a hill near by. They had discovered a fallen branch of an oak tree, and to this they had fastened a rope, pretending it was a plow, which one was holding as the others dragged it over the ground. Surprised at this curious implement and the small creatures, she gathered them all into her apron and ran home with them to her giant father. He, however, found no pleasure in the intended play-

---

* This legend is a complex of different giant stories localized at Puke Berg — Puke Mountain. Nearly every parish has its legend, in which the resident giant has been angered with the noise of the church bells, and has sought to destroy his disturber. The legend of the giantess who took the children from their plowing and bore them to her giant parent is not confined to the Giant Puke. Similar legends are current in Kläppe, in Oldesborg parish, in Dalland, etc.

Herman Hofberg

things but said only:

"Take them out again, our time is past; it is now these who shall rule over us."

In the end Puke became dissatisfied with everything and moved to Götland, where he was some time later found by a ship's master, to whom he gave a box, and bade him offer it upon the altar at Lofta while the people were in church, cautioning him strongly not to open it before.

"If you do as I bid you," said the Giant, "you will find, under the left fore-foot of Lofta's white mare—meaning the church—a key, with which you are to proceed to Puke Mountain. There you will see a door, which you shall open. When you are inside you will meet two black dogs. Do not be afraid of them, but press forward into the room, where you will find a table and upon it many beautiful silver vessels. Of them you may take the largest, but if you take anything more, misfortune will surely overtake you."

The captain kept this all in mind, but when he approached Puke Mountain, on his journey homeward, the conversation of the ship's people was turned to the box. After many deliberations, it was determined to throw it overboard onto a small island which lay near by. This was done, and upon the instant the island was in flames, and even to-day it is brown and desolate as if it had recently been swept by a fire.

Katrineholm Manor

In one of the picturesque valleys of romantic Småland and on the Black River is a noted waterfall called Stalpet, which, after placidly winding by many hundred bends, for a considerable distance through green meadows, here makes a precipitous descent over a rocky cliff, then quietly pursues its course to a lake a short distance beyond.

Not far from Stalpet lies an old manor, dark, gloomy and unoccupied. A feeling of oppression comes over one in the presence of this large building, barred gates and nailed up windows, and the question is asked, why should this naturally beautiful place be untenanted? Why is there not, at least, a watchman or an attendant? There must be some unusual reason for such a condition of things.

Let us listen to the narration of a good old woman, resident in the neighborhood, who once gave us the story. We use her words, which, may be, enter too much into the detail, but bear with them the natural freshness and coloring that, it is hoped, will not be tedious to the reader. We are given to understand that if we will have the story we must begin at the beginning, and that is, like "Milton's Paradise Lost," with the beginning of all things:

Know that when Satan was cast out of heaven, on account of his pride, and fell to the earth, there were other spirits, which, like him, were also cast out. These spirits, in their fall, were borne hither and thither on the winds like the golden leaves in the autumn storm, falling to earth finally, some into the sea, some into the forests and some upon the mountains. Where they fell there they remained, so the saying runs, and found there their field of action. After their abiding places they were given different names. Thus we have sea nymphs, mountain fairies, wood fairies, elves and other spirits, all of which are described in the catechism.

Now, it happened, that on that day two spirits fell upon the rock where this old Katrineholm Manor house now stands. In this mountain their offspring lived many hundreds, yes, thousands of years. Though some of them were from time to time killed by lightning and otherwise, they were not exterminated and had not been approached by any human being.

It happened, a long time ago, that a gentleman, who owned this estate, wishing to build himself a residence, and, like a wise architect, to have a solid foundation for it, selected this rock.

The Mountain King—for he was a king among his people—was very much displeased with this, but his wife, who was of a milder disposition, pacified her husband and urged him to wait and do their neighbors no harm until it could be known whether harm might be expected from them.

When the house was finished the gentleman married a beautiful young lady whose presence at once filled it with sunshine and joy. But sorrow visits many who little expect it and so it was here.

One day when the young wife was alone in her work-room, a little woman, unexpectedly and unannounced, stood before her. Bowing, she said: "My mistress bids that you visit her, and directs me to say to you that if you consent she will reward you richly." The young wife wondered much at such a request, but having a brave heart and a clear conscience, she promised to follow. The little woman led the way down stairs to the cellar, where she opened a door, until now undiscovered, revealing a passage into the mountain. Entering the passage, which was long and dark, she finally emerged into a large, well-lighted cave, whose walls were sparkling with gold and silver. Here, pacing back and forth, as if in great anguish, was a little man who looked at the newcomer searchingly, and with an humble and pleading expression in his eyes, but said nothing. The little woman pushed aside a curtain to an inner cave, at the further end of which the visitor saw, lying upon an elegant bed, another little woman sick and laboring in child-birth. The Christian visitor's presence had the effect to almost immediately still the pains of the suffering woman, whereupon she drew forth a box filled with precious stones, pearls and jewels. "Take this as a memento of your visit to me, but let none know what has happened to you this day, for as surely as you do great misfortune will overtake, you and yours," said the Mountain Queen, and directed that the young wife be given safe conduct to her room again. As soon as left alone the precious box was carefully secreted.

Time sped on. Everything went well, and in due time the young wife herself became the mother of two beautiful sons. One day, during the mother's absence, the boys discovered the secreted box, and had just begun to play with it when their father entered. He was greatly surprised to find such a treasure in the hands of the children and began at once to question the mother, who had also entered, as to how she became its possessor. At first she refused to betray the secret, and with her refusal the husband became more curious and suspicious, finally angry, when he declared his wife a Troll, and that he himself had seen her come riding through the air on a broomstick. The poor wife was then obliged to reveal her visit to the Troll queen and the circumstances attending it.

"You and I have seen our happiest days, for your curiosity will bring us greater misfortune than you have dreamed of," said she.

Herman Hofberg

A few days later there appeared in the adjacent lake an island, which, strangely enough, seemed to rise from its bosom when anything remarkable was about to take place. It is related that shortly before the death of Charles XII, also before that of Gustav III, the island became visible, and it is even said that a king one time carved his name on a stone on the island, and that stone and name, when, on another occasion the island was visible, were to be seen.

Whether the island was now again visible by some power of the Trolls in unison with the water spirits is not known; it is enough that the island appeared, and that the lord of the manor became possessed with a great desire to go to and inspect it.

He expressed a wish that his wife and boys should accompany him. The mother, who foresaw misfortune, opposed the project with all her energy, and upon her knees begged and prayed her husband to postpone his visit, but without avail.

Finally, the willful man took the boys, leaving his wife at home, and rowed out to the island. Just as the boat touched the enchanted island both boys sprang upon it, and at the same instant both island and boys vanished from the father's sight to be seen no more.

The poor mother mourned herself to death, and the father departed to foreign lands, where he also died, but the building on Katrinesholm has never since been occupied, and there is little probability that any one will in the future prosper in it.

Ebbe Skamelson[*]

Upon a small headland which juts from the north into Lake Bolmen, lies an old mansion, Tiraholm, by the peasantry called Tira. A long time ago there lived here a knight who had a wife and an only child, a beautiful daughter, named Malfred. In the whole country there was not another so fair, and the fame of her beauty traveled far and wide, alluring many suitors to her feet. But Malfred was unmoved by their attentions and turned them away, one after the other.

One day a stately knight, Ebbe Skamelson by name, who had just returned from foreign lands, where he had won his golden spurs, drew up in the courtyard. With downcast eyes and blushing cheeks the young lady extended her hand when they met, to greet the stranger, who courteously returned her salutation.

The stranger knight became for a time a guest at Tiraholm, and the report soon went out, to the grief of many swains who had indulged in dreams of sooner or later winning the hand of the beautiful maiden, that Ebbe Skamelson and Malfred were betrothed. But, as both were still young, the knight expressed a desire to join the Crusades to the Holy Land, where he hoped to add to his honors, and stipulated that he be given seven years, at the end of which time he promised to return and celebrate his nuptials.

Some time after Ebbe departed, the old knight, Malfred's father, died, and it became very lonesome for the daughter and mother in Tiraholm. Year after year passed with no word from Ebbe. The roses of the young maiden's cheeks faded and the dark eyes lost their lustre. The mother advised a remedy and betrothed her to another.

Under the impression that Ebbe had fallen by the sword of the infidels she prepared a wedding feast, and the newly betrothed couple were duly joined according to the rites of the church. But

[*] The same legend is also current in Halland, with the difference that Ebbe's lady love is said to have resided upon an estate in Tiveden, and that the remains of the exiled Knight now lie under a granite rock near the entrance to Gallinge Church.

just as the wedding guests sat themselves at table a gold-laced knight rode into the court at great speed. The bride became pale under her crown, but the mother, who recognized in the stranger the Knight Ebbe, hastened to meet him in the yard, and reminded him that the seven years had passed, at the same time informing him that his love now sat in the bridal chair with another.

In great anger the knight sprang to his horse, drew his sword, and after reproaching her for breaking her promise, with one blow he severed her head from her body. His sword still dripping with blood, he sprang from his saddle and into the hall where the festivities were in progress, where the bride sank under his sword, and the bridegroom at another deadly blow fell by her side.

Overtaken by repentance the murderer flung himself upon his horse and rode away into the dark forest, but the pricking of his conscience allowed him no rest. Night and day he saw the apparitions of his victims, and nowhere could he find an escape from them.

Finally he determined to go to Rome, and at the foot of the Holy Father ask absolution from his crimes. A large sum of money procured for him from the Pope the desired indulgence, but absolution from a man did not possess the power to quiet his conscience, still his soul's pain or quell the storm raging in his heart. He then returned to the home of his love, and asked the authorities to impose upon him the severest punishment.

After a long deliberation he was sentenced by the court to be chained hand and foot, in which condition he must visit and pass a day in each one of the three hundred and sixty-five islands in Lake Bolmen. The condemned man went at once about the execution of his sentence. In order that he might get from one island to the other he was given a small boat with which, like a wounded bird, he laboriously propelled himself on his terrible journey.

When, at the end of the year, his sentence was completed, he went ashore on the estate of Anglestadt in the district of Sunnebro. Here he went up to a village and rested over night in a barn. Meantime his sorrowful fate had made a deep impression upon the people. A bard had composed a song reciting the woes of

Ebbe, and a soothsayer had predicted that upon hearing the song sung Ebbe's chains would fall off and his death follow immediately. While he was lying concealed in the barn, a milkmaid came in the morning to milk the cows. She began to sing "Knight Ebbe's Song," to which he listened with intense interest. At the conclusion of the last verse he cried out with loud voice: "Some is true and some is false."

Thoroughly frightened, the girl sprang into the house and related what had happened. In great haste the people gathered around the barn where Ebbe was lying, commanding him to inform them where he came from and who he was. Still cumbered by his chains he crawled from his shelter and gave his name, at the same time requesting them to conduct him to the churchyard.

Between the village and the church of Angelstadt lies a stone sunken in the ground. When he came to this Ebbe mounted it, raised his eyes to heaven and cried out: "If I am worthy to be buried in consecrated ground, so let it be!"

Instantly the fetters fell from his hands and feet and he sank to the earth a corpse.

Those present took his body and carried it to the church where they buried it in the path outside the churchyard wall, so that all who went into the churchyard should tramp upon his grave. But the next night a long section of the wall, right in front of the grave, was miraculously thrown down. The peasants at once relaid it, but the next night it was again leveled. It was then understood that these happenings were signs that the unfortunate man should be allowed a resting place in consecrated ground, whereupon the churchyard was extended so that the grave was enclosed by its walls, and a low stone even to this day marks the resting place of the outcast. From the fetters, which for a long time hung in Anglestadt church, three iron crosses, resembling the small crosses which were in former times set up in memory of the departed, have been made and placed upon the present church.

Herman Hofberg

Johan and the Trolls*

In Ingeltrop, a parish of North Wedbo, there once lived a farmer who had a servant named Johan.

One day a traveler arrived from Myntorp Inn, and the farmer having been notified that it was his turn to furnish a conveyance for him to the next inn, Johan was sent to the pasture to catch a horse. A halter thrown over his shoulder, he set out, whistling the latest love song. Arriving at the pasture, it was soon clear to him that "Bronte" was in no humor to submit to the halter, and though he now and then allowed himself to be approached, no sooner was the attempt made to lay hold on him than he was off, with head and heels in the air, to a safe distance. Johan persevered, perspiration streaming from his forehead, but in vain. Angered at

* Before the days of railroads and regularly equipped stage lines, it was the duty, established by law, of the farmers and others owning horses to, in their turn, furnish travelers with means of conveyance from the inn of their neighborhood to the next. Upon the arrival of a traveler at an inn a servant was dispatched to the neighbor whose turn it was, and he was expected to promptly furnish horse, wagon and driver.

last, he began to swear in a most ungodly manner, still pursuing the horse until his progress was suddenly checked by a high cliff, to the very base of which he had run before discovering it. Naturally casting his glance upward, as he halted, he saw, sitting upon a crag, a beautiful maiden, apparently combing her hair.

"Are you there, my dear boy?" called the maiden.

Johan, not easily frightened, answered her cheerily:

"Yes, my sweetheart."

"Come here, then," called the maiden.

"I can't," replied Johan.

"Try, Johan." And he did, to his astonishment finding a foothold on the smooth cliff where before no unevenness was discoverable, and soon he was at the maiden's side. She looked at him with great, wondering eyes, then, suddenly enveloping him in a mist, clouded his understanding so that he was no longer master of his movements, and was, in fact, transformed completely from the Johan he had been, to a being like his companion. He forgot horse, home, relatives and friends. Half unconscious, he was conducted into the mountain, and was gone from the sight and power of those who would seek him.

"Bronte" was in harness many good days thereafter, and the farmer became the driver, for, as his sons were growing up, he did not wish to hire another servant in Johan's stead.

One day, many years after Johan's disappearance, it was again the farmer's turn to furnish a horse to a traveler. Grumbling at the fate of Johan, he went to the pasture.

"It was too bad for the boy," said he to himself. "I wonder if he has been caught by the Trolls?" At the same time he chanced to look upward at the cliff where the servant had seen the Troll maiden, and there stood Johan, but with lusterless eyes, staring into vacancy.

"Johan, my dear boy, is that you?" shouted the farmer. "Come down."

"I cannot," answered Johan, with husky, unnatural voice.

Hereupon the farmer threw his cap to Johan, which the latter picked up and put on his head.

Herman Hofberg

"Come down," cried the farmer, "before the Trolls come. In the name of the saints, come down."

"I can't," said Johan again.

Then the farmer threw his clothes up, garment after garment, and when Johan had clothed himself in them he received power enough that he was able to crawl down the cliff. His master took him by the hand, and without looking back they hastened home, the farmer repeating:

"Pshaw! You cunning black Trolls! As a stone, I'll quiet your wicked tongues that they may neither evil think nor speak or do ought against me."

They arrived home, the one dressed the other naked. The traveler was obliged to procure another horse, for in the house of the farmer the joy was so great that none there had a thought of driving him. Johan was never again the same man as before, but remained gloomy and rarely spoke.

His master asked him many times what his occupation was in the mountain, but upon this subject he was silent. It happened that Johan was taken sick and called for a confessor, to whom, when he confessed his sins, he related also his experience in the mountain. His chief employment, he said, had been to steal food for the Trolls. For this purpose the Trolls put a red hat upon him, when he could, in a very short time, fly to Jönkoping through locked doors and into the merchants' stores, where he took corn, salt, fish and whatever he wished. From the Troll cap he received such power that he could take a sack of rye under each arm and a barrel of fish upon his back, and fly as lightly through the air as with no burden whatever.

"It was wrong of me and hard on the merchants," said Johan, "but it was the fault of the Trolls. If there were no Trolls in the world the merchants would become rich, but now they must pay tribute, and so are kept on the verge of bankruptcy." And Johan was done.

The Lost Treasure

Many hundreds of years ago, at a time when Sweden was invaded by enemies, the people of Stenbrohult gathered their money and jewelry together and concealed them in a large copper kettle, which they sunk to the bottom of Lake Möckeln. There it lies to-day and will lie for all time, though many have touched it with poles when driving fish into their nets. Meantime, at each touch, it has moved further away until it now lies near the outlet of the lake, where it is so deep that it cannot be reached.

When the other residents of the place hid their treasures in the lake there was a rich farmer who buried his silver at Kalfhagsberg in two cans. Shortly after, he died so suddenly that no opportunity was given to dig them up. Immediately following his death, two lights were seen every evening over the place where the treasures lay hidden, a sure sign that an evil spirit or dragon had appropriated the treasure. A poor cottager heard of it, and knowing that man may acquire undisputed possession of the treasures of the earth, if dug up on a Thursday evening and carried away without looking back or uttering a word to anyone, he already regarded himself as good as the owner of the wealth. Betaking himself to the place, he succeeded in getting the cans out of the mountain, but on the way home he met one after another of his neighbors who asked where he had been. The old man knew well that the evil spirits had a hand in this, and that what appeared to be his neighbors was nothing less than the spirits transformed, and he was, therefore, stubbornly quiet. But finally he met the priest, who stood by the wayside and greeted him as he was passing with a "good evening, neighbor." Hereupon the old man dared keep quiet no longer, but took his hat off and saluted, "good evening, father," in return, at the same instant he tripped against a root and dropped the cans. When he stopped to pick them up there lay in their stead only a pair of little old birch-bark boxes, and the old man was compelled to go home, his mission fruitless.

Herman Hofberg

The Ten Fairy Servants[*]

Many years ago there lived in Gullbjers a family of peasants, who had a daughter, Elsa. As she was the only child she was much adored, and her parents sought in every way to anticipate

---

[*] An old Götland legend, by Madame D. Kindstrand, and in the *Family Journal*, elaborated by C. J. Bergman. Hop O' My Thumb, Lick the Pot, etc., are the names given the fingers.

her slightest wish. As soon as she had been confirmed she was sent to the city to learn how to sew, and also city manners and customs. But in the city she acquired little other knowledge than how to adorn herself, and to scorn housework and manual labor.

When she was twenty years old she won the love of an industrious and honorable young farmer, named Gunner, and before many months had gone by they were man and wife.

In the beginning all was pleasure, but she soon began to weary with her many household duties. Early one morning, shortly before Christmas, there was life and activity in Gunner's yard. Elsa had hardly risen from bed when the servant, Olle, sprang in and said:

"Dear mistress, get ready our haversacks, for we are going to the woods, and we must be off if we are to get back before evening."

"Dear mother, the leaven is working," called one of the servant girls, "and if you will come out now we will have more than usually good bread."

The butcher, Zarkis, who had already stuck a large hog and several small pigs, had just stepped in to get the accustomed dram, when old Brita came rushing after material for candle wicks. Lastly came Gunner, out of patience because the servant had not yet started for the woods.

"My departed mother," said he, with kindly earnestness, "always prepared everything the night before when people were expected to go to work early in the morning, and I have requested you to do likewise, Elsa. But do not forget the loom, my dear; there are now only a few yards of cloth remaining to be woven, and it will not do to allow it to lie in the way over the holidays."

Now, wholly out of patience, Elsa rushed in a rage out of the kitchen to the house in which the loom stood, slammed the door furiously behind her and cast herself weeping upon a sofa.

"No!" shrieked she. "I will no longer endure this drudgery. Who could have thought that Gunner would make a common housewife of me, to wear my life out thus? Oh, unhappy me! Is there no one who can help and comfort a poor creature?"

Herman Hofberg

"I can," replied a solemn voice, and before her stood a white-haired man with a broad-brimmed hat upon his head. "Do not be alarmed," continued he, "I came to proffer you the help for which you have just wished. I am called Old Man Hoberg. I know your family to the tenth and eleventh generations. Your first ancestor bade me stand godfather to his first born. I could not be present at the christening, but I gave a suitable godfather's present, for I would by no means be the meanest. The silver I then gave was unfortunately a blessing for no one, for it begot only pride and laziness. Your family long ago lost the riches, but the pride and laziness remain; nevertheless I will help you, for you are at heart good and honest.

"You complain at the life of drudgery you are compelled to lead," continued he, after a short silence. "This comes from your being unaccustomed to work, but I shall give you ten obedient servants, who shall be at your bidding and faithfully serve you in all your undertakings." Whereupon he shook his cloak, and ten comical little creatures hopped out and began to put the room in order.

"Reach here your fingers," commanded the old man.

Tremblingly, Elsa extended her hand; whereupon the old man said:

"Hop O' My Thumb,
"Lick the Pot,
"Long Pole,
"Heart in Hand,
"Little Peter Funny Man—
"Away, all of you, to your places."

In an instant the little servants had vanished into Elsa's fingers, and even the old man had disappeared.

The young wife sat a long time staring at her hands, but soon she experienced a wonderful desire to work.

"Here I sit and dream," she burst forth with unusual cheerfulness and courage, "and it is already seven o'clock while outside

Swedish Fairy Tales

all are waiting for me." And Elsa hastened out to superintend the occupations of her servants.

Not for that day alone, but for all time thereafter Elsa entered into her duties with as much pleasure as she would formerly have found in a dance. No one knew what had happened, but all marveled at the sudden change. None was, however, more pleased and satisfied than the young wife herself, for whom work was now a neccessity, and under whose hands everything thereafter flourished, bringing wealth and happiness to the young couple.

Herman Hofberg

The Sea Nymph

One night a number of fishermen quartered themselves in a hut by a fishing village on the northwest shores of an island. After they had gone to bed, and while they were yet awake, they saw a white, dew-besprinkled woman's hand reaching in through the door. They well understood that their visitor was a sea nymph, who sought their destruction, and feigned unconsciousness of her presence.

The following day their number was added to by the coming of a young, courageous and newly married man from Kinnar, in Lummelund. When they related to him their adventure of the night before, he made fun of their being afraid to take a beautiful woman by the hand, and boasted that if he had been present he would not have neglected to grasp the proffered hand.

That evening when they laid themselves down in the same room, the late arrival with them, the door opened again, and a plump, white woman's arm, with a most beautiful hand, reached in over the sleepers.

The young man arose from his bed, approached the door and seized the outstretched hand, impelled, perhaps, more by the fear of his comrades scoffing at his boasted bravery, than by any desire for a closer acquaintance with the strange visitor. Immediately his comrades witnessed him drawn noiselessly out through the door, which closed softly after him. They thought he would return soon, but when morning approached and he did not appear, they set out in search of him. Far and near the search was pursued, but without success. His disappearance was complete.

Three years passed and nothing had been heard of the missing man. His young wife, who had mourned him all this time as dead, was finally persuaded to marry another. On the evening of the wedding day, while the mirth was at its highest, a stranger entered the cottage. Upon closer observation some of the guests thought they recognized the bride's former husband.

The utmost surprise and commotion followed.

In answer to the inquiries of those present as to where he came from and where he had been, he related that it was a sea nymph whose hand he had taken that night when he left the fisherman's hut; and that he was dragged by her down into the sea. In her pearly halls he forgot his wife, parents, and all that was loved by him until the morning of that day, when the sea nymph exclaimed: "There will be a dusting out in Kinnar this evening." Then his senses immediately returned, and, with anxiety, he asked: "Then it is my wife who is to be the bride?" The sea nymph replied in the affirmative. At his urgent request, she allowed him to come up to see his wife as a bride, stipulating that when he arrived at the house he should not enter. When he came and saw her adorned with garland and crown he could, nevertheless, not resist the desire to enter. Then came a tempest and took away half the roof of the house, whereupon the man fell sick and three days later died.

Herman Hofberg

The Byse[*]

A peasant of Svalings, in the parish of Gothem, by the name of Hans, was, one spring day, employed in mending a fence which divided two meadows. It chanced he required a few more willow twigs for bands, whereupon he sprang over the fence to cut them in a neighbor's grove. Entering the thicket, what was his surprise at seeing an old man sitting upon a stump, bowed forward, his face buried in his hands. His astonishment uncontrollable, Hans broke out:

"Who are you?"

"A wanderer," replied the old man without lifting his head.

"How long have you been a wanderer?" inquired the peasant.

"Three hundred years!" answered the old man.

Still more astonished, the peasant again asked:

"Is it not hard to travel thus?"

"It has never been so hard to me," replied the old man, "for I love the woods."

"Very well, go on then," said Hans.

Hardly were the words uttered than the peasant heard a sound like that from a wild bird startled to wing, and the old man had vanished so suddenly that Hans could not say whether he had sunk into the earth or gone into the air.

---

* In Götland a Byse is the spirit of one who in life was continually on the move around his possessions, or was so covetous of worldly goods that even perjury did not deter him from acquiring property unjustly.

Swedish Fairy Tales

Bridge Over Kalmarsound

North of the village of Wi, in the parish of Källa, lies a large stone called Sekiel's Stone, after a giantess, Sekiel, who is said to have lived in Borgehaga, in the parish of Högo.

The same giantess had a sister, who was married to a giant named Beard, and lived in the parish of Ryssby on the Småland side of the sound.

That they might visit each other oftener it was agreed between the sisters that they should build a stone bridge over Kalmarsound, the one to build from Ryssby shore, the other from Öland.

The giantess of Småland began first upon her work. Every day she came with a great load of stones which she cast into the sea, until, finally, she had completed that point of land now called Skägganäs, reaching a quarter of a mile out into the sea. The giantess on the Öland side also began to build, but when she came with her first load of stones in her apron she was shot through the body with an arrow from a peasant's bow. Overcome by the pain, she sat herself to rest upon the before mentioned Sekiel Stone, which has a shallow depression in the top, marking the resting spot of the giantess.

When she had recovered she again took up her journey, but had proceeded no further than to Persnäs when it began to storm, and she was struck dead by a bolt of lightning. With her fall the stones slipped from her apron, and there they lie to-day, forming the large grave-mound on Persnäs hills.

The Young Lady of Hellerup

Upon the estate of Hellerup, in the parish of Ljungby, there lived, many years ago, a gentleman of rank, who had a daughter renowned for her gentleness as well as for her beauty and intelligence.

One night, while lying awake in her bed, watching the moonbeams dancing upon her chamber floor, her door was opened and a little fairy, clad in a gray jacket and red cap, tripped lightly in and toward her bed.

"Do not be afraid, gracious lady!" said he, and looked her in the eye in a friendly manner. "I have come to ask a favor from you."

"Willingly, if I can," answered the young lady, who began to recover from her fear.

"Oh! It will not be difficult," said the fairy. "I and mine have, for many years, lived under the floor in the kitchen, just where the water tank stands, which has become old and leaky, so that we are continually annoyed by the dripping of water, and the maids spill

Herman Hofberg

water upon the floor, which drips through, so that it is never dry in our home."

"That shall be seen to in the morning," promised the lady, and the fairy, making an elegant bow, disappeared as noiselessly as he came.

The next day, at the girl's request, the cask was moved, and the gratitude of the fairies was soon manifested. Never thereafter was a glass or plate broken, and if the servants had work to do that required early rising, they were always awake at the appointed hour.

Some time later the fairy again stood at the young lady's bed-side.

"Now I have another request which, in your generosity, you will certainly not refuse to grant."

"What is it, then?" asked the young lady.

"That you will honor me and my house, and tonight stand at the christening of my newly-born daughter."

The young lady arose and clad herself, and followed her un-known conductor through many passages and rooms which she had never before been aware existed, until she finally came to the kitchen. Here she found a host of small folk and priest and father, whereupon the little child was baptized in the usual Christian manner.

When the young lady was about to go the fairy begged permis-sion to put a memento in her apron.

Though what she received looked like a stick and some shav-ings, she appeared very thankful, and was conducted again through the winding passages back to her room.

Just as the fairy stood ready to leave her, he said: "If we should meet again, and that is probable, bear well in mind not to laugh at me or any of mine. We esteem you for your modesty and good-ness, but if you laugh at us, we shall never see each other again." With these words he left the room.

When he had gone the young woman threw her present into the stove and laid herself down to sleep, and the following morn-ing, when the maid went to build the fire, she found in the ashes jewelry of the purest gold and finest workmanship, such as had never before been seen.

Some years later the young woman was about to marry, and preparations were made for a day of pomp and splendor.

For many weeks there was great bustle in the kitchen and bridal chamber. During the day all was quiet under the floor in the kitchen, but through the night one who slept lightly could hear the sounds of work as through the day.

At length the wedding hour arrived.

Decked with laurels and crown, the bride was conducted to the hall where the guests were gathered. During the ceremonies she chanced to cast a glance toward the fireplace in the corner of the hall, where she saw the fairies gathered for a like feast. The bridegroom was a little fairy and the bride her goddaughter, and everything was conducted in the same manner as in the hall.

None of the guests saw what was going on in their vicinity, but it was observed that the bride could not take her eyes from the fireplace. Later in the evening, when she again saw the strange bridal feast, she saw one of the fairies who was acting as waiter stumble and fall over a twig. Unmindful of the caution she had received, she burst out into a hearty laugh. Instantly the scene vanished, and from that time no fairies have been seen at Hellerup.

Elstorps Woods

During the war between Queen Margarita and Albrecht of Mecklenburg the two armies had an encounter in Southern Halland. The Queen's people had encamped upon the plains of Tjarby, a half mile north of Laholm, while the Prince's adherents were camped in the vicinity of Weinge Church.

One morning the Queen went, as was her custom, to morning prayers in Tjarby Church, but took the precaution to set a guard upon the so-called Queen's Mountain to warn her of danger.

While she was buried in her devotions there came a message, informing her that a few unattended knights had been seen in the vicinity.

"There is yet no danger," said the courageous Queen, and continued her prayers at the altar.

In a short time another message was brought, informing her that as many as a hundred knights had made their appearance, but the Queen commanded her people to keep still, that yet there was no occasion for alarm. Finally a message came that all Elstorps Woods seemed to be alive and moving against Tjarby.

"Now, my children, for a hard battle, but God will give us the victory," said the Queen, and springing upon her horse, she marched at the head of her warriors against the enemy.

The enemy had, as is related in the story of Macbeth, made use of stratagem, for each man carried before him a green bush, thinking to come upon the queen's attendants by surprise. But the queen outwitted him and gained a brilliant victory.

In gratitude to God, she rebuilt the old church of Tjarby, and since that day no birches higher than a man's head have grown in Elstorps Woods.

Pigmy of Folkared's Cliff

It is probable that there are few places more gloomy and uninviting than certain parts of the parish of Sibbarp, in the Province of Halland. Dark heaths cover a good portion of the parish, and from their dull brown surface rises, here and there, a lonely, cheerless mountain. One of these is Folkared's Cliff, in the southern part of the parish, noted of old as the abiding-place of little Trolls and Pigmies.

Herman Hofberg

One chilly autumn day a peasant, going from Hogared, in Ljungby, to Folkared, in Sibbarp, in order to shorten his journey took a short cut by way of the cliff, upon reaching which he perceived a Pigmy about the size of a child seven or eight years old, sitting upon a stone crying.

"Where is your home?" asked the peasant, moved by the seeming distress of the little fellow.

"Here," sobbed the Pigmy, pointing to the mountain.

"How long have you lived here?" questioned the peasant in surprise.

"Six hundred years."

"Six hundred years! You lie, you rascal, and you deserve to be whipped for it."

"Oh! Do not strike me," pleaded the Pigmy, continuing to cry. "I have had enough of blows already to-day."

"Who have you received them from?" asked the peasant.

"From my father."

"What capers did you cut up that you were thus punished?"

"Oh, I was set to watch my old grandfather and when I chanced to turn my back he fell and hurt himself upon the floor."

The peasant then understood what character of person he had met, and grasping his dirk he prepared to defend himself. But instantly he heard an awful crash in the mountain, and the Pigmy had vanished.

The Freebooter's Grave

During the bloody war under Charles XII with Denmark, a number of freebooters had gone from Skåne into Halland, and marked their way, as usual, with plundering and murder. A number, after the parsonage and other houses in Hishult had been ransacked, went back to Skåne; the rest continued their course to the north.

At Böghult, in the parish of Tönnersjö, a number of peasants had gathered to oppose them. They possessed, for the most part, no other weapons than axes, scythes and sticks; only two, brothers from Böghult, were better armed. Each of these had his gun, which, as residents in the woods and hunters, they knew well how to handle. In stationing the forces, the two brothers were placed far out on the road, in the direction from which the freebooters were expected to make their appearance, while the others remained in a body some distance in their rear.

After many hours' waiting a ragged, sorry-looking horseman, mounted on a rough-coated and saddleless horse, came into view. From his rear came the sounds of laughter and merry-making of the approaching horde.

"Look sharp! Here they come!" said one of the brothers.

"See! They have stolen father's horse!" said the other, as he brought his gun to his eye.

"Hold on!" whispered the first. "My gun is surer than yours. Let me take care of the thief." These words were followed by a loud report, and the horseman tumbled from his seat.

Alarmed at the result, the two brothers retreated hastily to their support in the rear, and nothing further was heard of the enemy. The following day some of the bravest of the peasants set out to reconnoiter, but the freebooters had disappeared. They came, however, upon a heap of stones which the marauders had thrown up to mark the grave of their companion.

This pile of stones was ever after called the freebooter's grave.

Herman Hofberg

The Giant Maiden

In the mountain of Boraserod, which is located in the parish of Svarteborg, there lived, in ancient days, a giant. As with all the giant people, he has disappeared since the coming in of Christianity. Some say that he died, but others believe that he moved to Dovre, in Norway, where giants betook themselves when disturbed by the church bells.

However, there is even to-day a hollow in the mountain which is called "the giant's door," and within the mountain, it is believed there are vaults filled with the giant's gold. No one has, however, dared venture to search for this treasure, and luckily, for with property of giants, blessings do not go.

This giant had a daughter, so beautiful that he who once saw her could never drive thoughts of her from his mind. Among the few whose fortune it was to see her was a young peasant from the estate of Rom, adjacent to the mountain. When he was one day out searching for the horses, which had gone astray, he suddenly came upon the wonderfully beautiful maiden, sitting upon the side of the mountain, in the sunshine, playing on her harp.

The peasant at once understanding who it was, not of the kind to be easily frightened, knowing that her father had an abundance of riches, and thinking it was no worse for him than for many others to marry into the giant family, approached her, under cover of the shrubbery, until he was quite near, when he threw his knife between her and the mountain, and as "steel charms a Troll," or others of the supernatural family, she was obliged, whether or not she would, to follow him to his home.

In the evening, when the giant missed his daughter, he started out in search of her, and in his search came to Rom. Through the walls he heard the snores of two persons, and, when he had lifted the roof off the cottage, he saw his daughter sleeping in the arms of the young swain.

"Are you there, you whelp!" he hissed. "Has it come to this?" added he. "So be it, then; but I demand that the wedding shall take place before the next new moon. If you can then give me as much

food and drink as I want all your offspring shall be made rich and powerful, otherwise I will have nothing to do with you."

Preparations were hastily made by the young man's parents for the wedding, and neighbors and relations came from far and near, laden with provisions. A great number likely to be present, it was determined to have the ceremony performed in the Church of Tosse; but the day before the wedding there came such a great freshet that it seemed impossible for the bridal carriage to cross the swollen creek between Duigle and Barby. The giant was equal to the emergency, and, with his wife, went to Holmasar, in Berffen-dalen, and fetched a large slab of stone and four boulders to the creek. The giant carried the slab under his arm, and his wife the

Herman Hofberg

boulders in her mitten. And thus they built the stone bridge which to this day spans the creek.

When the bridal pair came from the church to the banquet hall, the giant appeared and seated himself at the table with the rest of the guests.

Although the bridal couple did all possible to find him enough to eat, the giant declared when he left the table that he was only half satisfied, and therefore only half of the family should become great people. Wishing to give the bride a becoming bridal present, he cast a sack of gold and silver upon the floor, which the couple was to have if the son-in-law could carry it up to the loft. Stealthily, the bride gave her husband a drink which made him so strong that he threw the sack upon his back, and, to the surprise of all, carried it out of the room. Thus the newly wedded pair became possessors of an abundant treasure with which to begin life.

For some time the young couple lived in plenty and happiness, but soon the husband began to be irritable and abusive. It came, finally, to such a pass that the husband took a whip to his wife. She continued, nevertheless, to be mild and patient as before; but one day he was about to start on a long journey. When the horse was hitched to the wagon he observed that the shoe was gone from one of the hind feet. It would not do to venture on such a journey without first replacing the shoe. Here, however, was a difficulty. He had one shoe only, and that was too large; whereupon he began again to scold and swear.

The wife said nothing, but quietly taking the shoe between her hands, squeezed it together as if it were lead, reducing it to the required size. Her husband looked upon her in astonishment and alarm. Finally he addressed her:

"Why have you, who are so strong, submitted to abuse from me?"

"Because the wife should be submissive to her husband," said the giantess, mildly and pleasantly.

From that hour the man was the most patient and indulgent in the region, and never again was heard a cross word from his mouth.

Gloshed's Altar*

South of Thorsby Church, among the mountains, lies a shattered rock called Gloshed's Altar, concerning which there is an old tradition still living upon the lips of the people, as follows:

A long time ago a man from the parish of Säfve went upon a Hollandish ship, on a whaling cruise. After the vessel had been tossed about the sea for some time, land was one day sighted, and upon the land was seen a fire which continued to burn many days.

It was determined that some of the ship's crew should go ashore, in the hope that shelter might be found, and among those who went ashore was our hero. When the strand was reached they found there an old man sitting by a fire of logs, endeavoring to warm himself.

"Where did you come from?" asked the old man.

"From Holland!" answered the sailors.

"But where were you born?" to our hero.

"In Hisingen, in the parish of Säfve," he answered.

"Are you acquainted in Thorsby?"

"Yes, indeed!"

"Do you know where Ulfve Mountain lies?"

"I have often passed it, as the road from Göteborg to Marstrand over Hisingen and through Thorsby goes past there."

"Do the large stones and hills remain undisturbed?" asked the old man.

"Yes, except one stone, which, if I remember correctly, is toppling over," said the Hisinger.

"That is too bad! But do you know where Gloshed's Altar is, and does it remain sound?"

"Upon that point," said the sailor, "I have no knowledge."

Finally the old man continued: "If you will say to those who now live in Thorsby and Torrebräcka that they shall not destroy

---

* In Bohusländ and in Dalland the belief is quite general that the giants, leaving those regions, settled upon Dovre in Norway, or upon some uninhabited island in the North Sea, and that travelers are eagerly questioned about their former home.

Herman Hofberg

the stones and elevations at the foot of Ulfve Mount, and, above all, to take care of Gloshed's Altar, you shall have fair winds for the rest of your voyage."

The Hisinger promised to deliver the message when he arrived home, whereupon he asked the old man his name, and how he, living so far from Thorsby, was so well acquainted with matters there.

"I'll tell you," said he, "my name is Thore Brock, and I at one time lived there, but was banished. All my relations are buried at Ulfve Mountain, and at Gloshed's Altar we were wont to do homage to our gods and to make our offerings."

Hereupon they separated.

When the man from Hisinger returned home he went about the fulfillment of his promise, and, without knowing how, he soon became one of the principal farmers in the parish.

The Bridal Present

In the parish of Näsinge, two poor sisters once found service with a rich farmer. All through the summer they herded their master's flocks on the mountain sides, whiling away their time in relating legends of kings and abducted princesses.

"If only some prince would carry me away to his gilded palace," said the younger, one day.

"Hush! Do not talk so wickedly," remonstrated the elder. "The Trolls might hear you, when it would go hard with you."

"Oh! There is not much danger of that," replied the first speaker, and continued her story.

Some days later the younger sister disappeared. No one knew where she had gone, and careful search did not reveal. Time went on without the least trace of her whereabouts being discovered. Finally the remaining sister found a sweetheart, but equally poor with herself, wherefore they could not think of marrying yet for many years. One night in her sleep she dreamed that her absent sister stood at her bedside, and said: "Make your bed to-morrow night in the barn, past which the Trolls and I shall pass, and I will give you a handsome dower."

The next night when the girl drove her flocks home she made her bed, as her sister had directed, in her master's barn. The barn door she left open, and, laying herself down, she looked out into the night, endeavoring to keep awake until her sister should come. Soon after midnight she heard the sound of hoofs, and saw her sister, accompanied by a Troll, ride up the road at such a speed that the sparks glistened around the horses' feet. When they reached the front of the barn the lost girl threw a purse in at the door, which fell with a ring into the watcher's lap. Hastily the treasure was deposited under her head, and she was soon asleep, wearied with her day's work and night of watching. The next day, upon examining her strange gift, what was her astonishment to find it filled with gold coins. Before the sun had set she had purchased a splendid farm, and, as may be presumed, the bans were published and a wedding immediately celebrated.

Herman Hofberg

The Hålde Hat*

At the extremity of the beautiful valley of Espelund, in the parish of Mo, there rises a woodcovered mountain known as Bergåsa Mountain, from the distance looking like a giant cone; three sides presenting frowning precipices, the fourth (and southern) fortified by a large wall of boulders, which is said to have surrounded, in former times, a king's castle, called Grimslott. Here, in

---

* The belief that Giants have two hats, one of which renders the wearer invisible, and another that reveals things otherwise invisible, is widespread in Northern Scandinavia.

Swedish Fairy Tales

times gone by, lived a mountain king named Grim. He was, like the rest of his kind, ugly and crafty, and robbed mankind of whatever fell in his way. For this purpose he had two hats, one of which was called the Dulde hat, and was so endowed that when the king put it on his head both he and his companions became invisible; and the other was called the Hålde hat, which possessed a power making all things visible to the wearer that were before invisible.

It happened, during these days, that a farmer of Grimland, preparing a wedding for his daughter, invited guests from near and far to the festivities. Pretending, however, not to know the mountain king, he did not invite him. The latter apparently took no offense at this, but, on the wedding day, putting his Dulde hat upon his head, set out to the wedding feast, followed by all his people, except the queen, who was left at home to watch the castle.

When the wedding guests sat themselves at table everything that was brought in vanished, both food and drink, to the great astonishment of all, as they could not understand where it disappeared; but a young peasant suspected the Trolls were at the bottom of it, and, springing upon a horse, rode straightway to Borgåsa Mountain. On the steps stood the mountain queen, so beautiful and fine, who inquired of the rider how things were going at the wedding feast in Grimland.

"The food is salt and the oil is sour," answered he. "That stingy farmer has hidden the wine and meat in the cellar where no one can find it. Now, your husband sends greeting, and requests that you give me the Hålde hat, that he may find its hiding place."

Without mistrust the queen gave him the enchanted hat, whereupon the young peasant hastened back to the festivities. Entering the hall, he donned the hat and saw at once the mountain king and his followers sitting among the guests, seizing upon everything as fast as brought in. The peasant drew his sword, and commanded the others to do likewise.

"Stab as I stab and cut as I cut," cried he, and began to slash around the table. The other guests followed his example and slew the mountain king and all his followers. From that time, so says the story, the castle upon Borgåsa Mountain has been untenanted.

Herman Hofberg

The Golden Cradle

One stormy autumn night, a few years after the death of Charles XII, a ship containing a valuable cargo was wrecked on the island of Tjorn, one of the group of islands on the coast of Bohuslän. Among other things of value in the ship's cargo were many articles of costly jewelry, belonging to King Frederick I, which were being brought to him from Hessia. The most costly, however, was a jewel enclosed in a cradle made of pure gold and richly embellished with pearls and precious stones, sent by a German princess to the king's spouse.

The islanders, as was not unusual in those days, murdered the ship's crew, and, after it had been plundered of its cargo, scuttled and sunk her, so that she was safely out of sight.

Among the priests upon the island was one named Michael Koch, pastor in Klofvedal. He had a hint of the great crime that had been committed, but, fearing the half-barbarous inhabitants, did not dare betray the secret.

Some time after the ship had disappeared a fisherman came one day to the parsonage and presented to the priest a walking stick of great beauty of workmanship and value, which was a part of the cargo of the plundered vessel. Koch accepted the gift, and whether he did not know or did not care where it came from, took it with him, often displaying it upon the streets. When, two years later, he went to Stockholm, as representative to the Diet, King Frederick one day accidentally saw and recognized it as his property. The priest, however, asserted that it was his, and rightfully acquired. But the king could not be deceived, and opening a heretofore concealed hollow in the cane, took therefrom a roll of gold coins. This action attracted attention and aroused suspicion anew that the ship had been plundered. It was not thought that Koch had a hand in it, but, on the assumption that he knew something about it which he ought to have revealed, and that he was trying to conceal the deed, he was escorted from Stockholm.

Meantime further discoveries were made, until they led to finding that the gold cradle was in possession of a peasant in

Stordal. At the king's command, soldiers were at once dispatched to Tjorn to arrest the criminals and, possibly, find the jewel. But the command was not kept so secret that the peasant did not get an intimation of what was coming, whereupon he hastened to bury the cradle in Stordal Heath. Under guidance of a police officer the search was prosecuted in all directions, but when the soldiers could not discover the object of their search, they left the island and the offenders escaped.

Some years later the possessor of the cradle became sick. When he found that his case was serious he sent for the priest, and confided to him the whereabouts of his booty, and requested that as soon as he was dead the priest should dig the cradle up and restore it to the king. Hardly had the priest taken his departure when the sick man regretted his simplicity. Gathering his little remaining strength, he rose from his bed, and, with unsteady steps, crept out into the field and concealed his buried treasure in another place. As soon as the man was dead, the priest set out about fulfilling his commission. His digging was in vain, the hidden treasure was not to be found. In his dying hour the peasant had, apparently, endeavored to reveal the new hiding place, but his strength was so near exhausted that his utterances could not be understood.

To this day many of the dwellers on the island are fully persuaded that Queen Elenor's golden cradle may be found somewhere in the Stordal cow pastures, and many have wasted much time and labor in the hope of bringing it to light.

Herman Hofberg

The Child Phantom

Many years ago there died, on the estate of Sundshult, in the parish of Nafverstad, a child of illegitimate birth, which, because of this, was not christened and could not be accorded Christian burial, or a place in heaven, and whose spirit, therefore, was left to wander the earth, disturbing the rest and making night uncomfortable for the people of the neighborhood.

One time, just before Christmas, the parish shoemaker, on his rounds, was detained at the house of a patron, and, having much work before him, he was still sewing late into the night, when he was unexpectedly startled from his employment by a little child appearing before him, which said:

"Why do you sit there? Move aside."

"For what?" asked the shoemaker.

"Because I wish to dance," said the spectre.

"Dance away, then!" said the shoemaker.

When the child had danced some time it disappeared, but returned soon and said:

"I will dance again, and I'll dance your light out for you."

"No," said the shoemaker, "let the light alone. But who are you that you are here in this manner?"

"I live under the lower stone of the steps to the porch."

"Who put you there?" asked the shoemaker.

"Watch when it dawns, and you will see my mother coming, wearing a red cap. But help me out of this, and I'll never dance again."

This the shoemaker promised to do, and the spectre vanished.

The next day a servant girl from the neighboring estate came, who wore upon her head a red handkerchief.

Digging was begun under the designated step, and in time the skeleton of a child was found, encased in a wooden tub. The body was that day taken to the churchyard, and the mother, who had destroyed her child, turned over to the authorities. Since then the child spectre has danced no more.

Herman Hofberg

King Rane and Queen Hudta

Upon the height where Svarteborg's Church is now situated, rose, in former times, a castle, occupied at the date of our story by a king named Rane, after whom the fortification took the name of Ranesborg. As late as a few years ago traces of a wall were to be seen in the so-called bell-tower, near the church path, which were said to be the remains of the once stately fortress.

At the time King Rane resided in Ranesborg, there lived not far from there, upon the Hudt estate, in the parish of Tanum, a Queen Hudta, widely known for her wealth and beauty, also for her rare bravery and sour temper.

Enraptured by the king's fame for bravery, though well along in years, she sent an ambassador to the king offering him her hand, which he accepted. After a time he fell in love with another and regretted his previous betrothal, but said nothing to Queen Hudta, who, upon the appointed day, betook herself, arrayed in queenly garb and glittering crown, to Ranesborg.

When the bridal car arrived at the castle it was found that the king had gone on a hunt, and had left word that the queen might return to her home again. Stung by this bitter affront, the queen commanded her people to storm the castle and raze it to the ground. Returning to her horse, when the destruction had been completed, and viewing the black and smoking ruins of the castle, she thus vented herself:

"Up to the present you have been called Ranesborg, but hereafter you shall be known as Svarteborg" — Black Castle — and, putting spurs to her horse, she galloped away from the spot.

When the queen came to the so-called Köpstadbäcken, on her way to Tanum, she halted at a spring, dismounted and laid her crown and equipments upon a stone. She then requested a drink, and, the water being good, the spring was named Godtakällan — good spring. Meantime Rane, during the chase, had observed the smoke and flames from his burning castle and set out hastily homeward. At Köpstadbäcken he came upon the bridal car of the malevolent queen, when he understood what had taken place, and drawing his sword, he clove the head of his intended bride. At sight of this her followers at once took to flight, but they were overtaken and hewn down at Stenehed, where one of the finest monuments on Bohuslän marks the incident. The murdered queen's body was carried to her castle at Hudt, where a large prostrate stone near the wagon road is said to mark her grave.

Herman Hofberg

The Knights of Ållaberg

One time a peasant, en route to Jönköping with a load of rye, came just at dusk to Ållaberg, where he discovered a grand mansion by the way. "Maybe I can sell my rye here," thought he, "and so be spared the journey to Jönköping," and, approaching the door, he knocked for admittance.

The door was at once opened by some unseen power, and the peasant entered.

Upon entering, he found himself in a grand hall. In the middle of the floor stood a large table and upon the table lay twelve golden helmets, grand beyond the power of description, and scattered around the room, deep in slumber, were twelve knights in glittering armor.

The peasant contemplated his beautiful surroundings, but, concluding he could not sell his rye here, went on, coming finally to a large stable, where he found standing twelve most magnificent steeds, bedecked with golden trappings and silver shoes on their hoofs, stamping in their stalls.

90

Curiosity getting the better of him, he took hold of the bridle of one of the horses in order to learn by what art it was made. Hardly had he touched it when he heard a voice call out, "Is it time now?" and another answer, "No, not yet!"

The peasant had now seen and heard as much as he desired, and, thoroughly frightened, hastened away. When he came out he found that he had been into the mountain instead of into a mansion, and that he had seen the twelve knights who sleep there until the country shall be in some great danger, when they will awake and help Sweden to defend herself against her foreign enemies.

Herman Hofberg

The Countess of Höjentorp[*]

Shortly after King Charles XI had confiscated most of the property of the nobility to the use of the crown, he came, one day, while upon one of his journeys to Höjentorp, where his aunt on his father's side, Maria Eufrosyna, lived.

On the stairs, as he was about to enter her dwelling, he was met by her and at once saluted with a sound box on the ear. Astounded, the king burst out:

"It is fortunate that it is I whom you have struck! But why are you in such a combative mood, my aunt?"

"Why?" said the countess. "Because you have taken all my possessions from me."

Conducting the king to the dining hall, the countess sat before him to eat a herring's tail and an oat cake.

"Have you no better fare for me than this?" asked the king.

"No," replied the lady; "as you have spread the cloth so must you dine."

"Aunt," said the king, "if you will give me your gold and silver, I will provide for you richly to your death."

"Shame on you!" interrupted the countess. "Will you not allow me to keep so little as my gold and silver, either?" and, advancing upon him, she gave him a second box on the ear, which so alarmed the king that he beat a hasty retreat and commanded that the countess be left in peaceful possession of her property to the end of her days.

---

* This legend is noteworthy as showing how time and fancy often clothe the historical fact in mythical garb. The reader's attention is called to similar cases in this collection, among them the *Lord of Ugerup, Bishop Svedborg and the Devil, Lady Barbro of Brokind, Jonas Spits,* etc.

Swedish Fairy Tales

The Giant of Skalunda

On Skalunda Hill, near Skalunda Church, there lived, in olden times, a giant, who, much annoyed by the ringing of the church bells, was finally compelled to move away, and took up his residence on an island, far away in the North Sea. One time a ship was wrecked upon this island, and among those of her crew rescued were several men from Skalunda.

"Where are you from?" inquired the giant, who was now old and blind, and was stretched out warming himself before a fire of logs.

"We are from Skalunda, if you wish to know," said one of the men.

"Give me your hand, for I wish to know if still there is warm blood in Sweden," said the giant.

The man, afraid of the grasp of the giant, drew a glowing iron rod from the fire, which he extended to the giant, who, grasping it with great force, squeezed it until the iron ran between his fingers.

"Ah, yes, there is still warm blood in Sweden," exclaimed he, "but does Skalunda Hill still exist?"

"No, the birds have scratched it down," answered the man.

"It could not stand," remarked the giant, "for my wife and daughter built it one Sunday morning. But how is it with Halle and Hunneberg? They remain, surely, for I myself built them."

Upon receiving a reply in the affirmative, he asked if Karin, a giantess, still lived, and when to this he was answered yes, he gave them a belt and bade them take it to Karin and say to her that she must wear it in his memory.

The men took the belt, and upon their return home gave it to Karin, but, before she would put it upon herself, she wrapped it around an oak which was growing near by. Hardly was this done when the oak was torn from the ground, and sailed off northward as if in a gale. In the ground where the oak stood, there was left a deep pit, and here to-day is pointed out the best spring in Stommen.

The Trolls in Resslared

In a mountain called Räfvakullen, Fox Hill, near the Church of Resslared, Trolls, it is said, have lived since long before the building of the church.

When the church was completed and the bell hung in the tower, the priest, as was the custom, proceeded to read prayers over it to protect it from the power of the Trolls. But his prayers lacked the expected efficacy, for he had not yet finished when the Trolls took the bell and sunk it in the "Troll Hole" near the church.

A new bell was cast and hung, and this time the provost, who was more learned, was selected to consecrate it. The provost also failed to hit upon the right prayers, for the following Sunday, when the bell was about to be used for the first time, it flew through the apertures in the tower and was broken on the roof of the church.

Again a bell was cast, and this time, as priest and provost seemed to be powerless against the Trolls, the Bishop of Skara was sent for. His prayers were effectual, and the bell was not again disturbed.

The Trolls thereafter dwelt in harmony with their neighbors, and especially with the parishioners of Resslared. From the latter the Trolls were wont to borrow food and drink, which they always returned two-fold.

In time the first residents died off, and new people took their places. The newcomers were well provided with this world's goods, even to being wealthy, but they were niggardly and uncharitable.

One day the "mother" of the Trolls went, as was her custom of old, to a cottage, and asked the housewife if she could lend her a measure of meal.

"No, that is out of the question! I have none in the house!" said the woman.

"Very well! It is as you say, of course," replied the Troll, "but maybe you can lend me a can or two of ale. My husband is away, and he will be very thirsty when he returns."

"No, I can't do that. My ale cans are all empty," answered the housewife.

"Very good! Maybe you can lend me a little milk for my little child that is sick in the mountain."

"Milk! Where should I get milk? My cows are all farrow," said the woman.

"Very well," said the Troll woman, and went her way.

The housewife laughed in her sleeve, and thought that she had escaped the Trolls cheaply; but when she inspected her larder it was found that she had really told the truth to the Troll woman. The meal boxes were swept clean, the ale barrels were empty, and the new milch cows, to the last one, farrow. Ever after that the plenty that had heretofore been was wanting, until finally the people were compelled to sell out and move away.

Bishop Svedberg and the Devil

Bishop Svedberg, of Skara, was a very pious man and a mighty preacher, therefore, intolerable to the devil.

One night the Bishop set out from Skara to his bishopric in Brunsbo. When he was on the way some distance, the wagon began to run from side to side of the road, and finally one of the hind wheels fell off and rolled away into the ditch.

The driver called the attention of the Bishop to this, and remarked that they could go no farther.

"Don't trouble yourself about that," said the Bishop. "Throw the wheel into the rear of the wagon and we will go along."

The servant thought this a strange command, but did as directed, and the journey was continued to Brunsbo without fur-

Herman Hofberg

ther adventure.

Arriving at the inn, the Bishop directed the servant to go to the kitchen and bring a light.

"Look, now," said the Bishop to the servant upon his return, "and you shall see who has been the fourth wheel," at the same time springing from the wagon.

The servant turned the light in the direction indicated, where he saw none other than the devil himself, standing in the place of the wheel, with the axle in his hands.

The devil soon found an opportunity for revenge. One night a great fire spread over Brunsbo, and before morning the whole place was burned to the ground.

The Bishop was at no loss to know who had played him this foul trick, and called the devil to account for the devastation.

"Verily, you shall know," said the devil. "Your maid was down in the pantry, and there snuffed the candle. Passing by, I took the snuffing and with it set fire to the place."

The Bishop was obliged to be content with this answer, but in order that the devil should do him no further harm he sent him, with all his imps, to hell.

The Treasure in Säby Creek

On the estate of Säby, in the parish of Hassie, lived, in former days, a gentleman so rich that he could have purchased half of the territory of Vestergötland, but so miserly that he could not find it in his heart to spend money for necessary food.

When he became aged, and knew that his life was drawing to a close, he began to ponder what he should do with his wealth to prevent its falling into the hands of people not akin to him, and finally he arrived at what he thought a wise determination.

One Sunday, when the people of the house were all in church, he loaded his gold and silver upon a golden wagon and drew it down to Säby Creek, where he sank it in the deepest hole he could find. Reaching home again, he felt more than usually content, and laid himself down upon his bed, where he was found upon the return of the people from church.

When a treasure has been concealed seven years, the Red Spirit is said to take possession of it, and it is then called "Dragon's property." Over the spot where the treasure lies a blue flame is seen to flutter at night time, and it is said the dragons are then polishing their treasure.

When the seven years had passed the dragon light was seen over Säby Creek, now for the first time revealing where the miser had deposited his wealth. Many efforts were made to recover the costly wagon and its load, but neither horses nor oxen were found with strength enough to lift it from the hole.

About this time it happened that a farmer, returning from the market of Skagersholm, where he had been with a load of produce, found quarters for the night with an old man at Tveden. The evening conversation turned upon the hidden treasure, and the many unsuccessful attempts to recover it that had been made, when the old man instructed his guest to procure a pair of bull calves, upon which there should not be a single black hair, and to feed them for three years on skimmed milk, whereby they would acquire the necessary strength to drag the wagon out of the creek.

Herman Hofberg

After great trouble the farmer was fortunate enough to find the desired white calves, and he at once set about rearing them as instructed. But one time the girl who had care of the calves accidentally spilled some of the milk set apart for one of them, and, in order to have the pail full, she replaced the milk with water and gave it to the calf as if nothing had happened. Meantime the calves grew up on their excellent food to large and powerful oxen.

When they were three years old the farmer drove them to the creek and hitched them to the golden wagon. It was heavy, but the calves put their shoulders to it, and had raised it half way from the hole, when one of them fell upon his knees, and the wagon sank back to its old resting-place. The farmer yoked them to it again, but just as the wagon was about to be landed safely, the same bull fell to its knees a second time, so it went time after time, until, finally, the owner saw that one of the bulls was weaker than the other.

When the wagon sank back the last time a bubbling and murmuring came up from the depths and a smothered voice was heard to mutter:

"Your skimmed milk calves can't draw my wagon out." Whereupon the farmer understood that to trouble himself further would be useless, since when no attempts have been made to secure the treasure.

The Tomts*

In descriptions of Tomts we are told that they look like little men well along in years, and in size about that of a child three or fours years old, as a rule clad in coarse gray clothes and wearing red caps upon their heads. They usually make the pantry or barn their abidingplace, where they busy themselves night and day, and keep watch over the household arrangements. When the servants are to go to threshing, or other work requiring early rising, they are awakened by the Tomts. If there is building going on, it is a good sign if the Tomts are heard chopping and pounding during the hours of rest for the workmen. In the forge where the Tomts have established themselves, the smith may take his rest in confidence that they will awaken him by a blow on the sole of the foot when it is time for him to turn the iron. Formerly no iron was worked on "Tomt night," which they reserved for purposes of their own. On this night, were one to peek through the cracks of the door, the little people would be discovered working silver bars, or turning their own legs under the hammer.

It is believed that in the house or community where there is order and prosperity the Tomts are resident, but in the house where proper respect is lacking, or where there is a want of order and cleanliness, they will not remain, and it will follow that the cup-board and corn-crib will be empty, the cattle will not thrive, and the peasant will be reduced to extreme poverty and want.

It happened thus to a farmer that he had never finished his threshing before spring, although he could not find that he had harvested more grain than others of his neighbors. To discover, if might be, the source of such plenty, he one day hid himself in the

---

* The belief in Tomts has been handed down to us through many generations, and is widespread in Sweden. In the opinion of the writer they are nothing more or less than an inheritance from the classical past and a remnant of the domestic worship which the ancients bestowed upon their family gods. Legends similar to this are related in Norway, where the spirit is called Topvette or Tomlevette and Gardos; also in Faroe Islands, where they are called Niagriusar, and in Germany, where they are called Kobolde, etc.

barn, whence he saw a multitude of Tomts come, each bearing a stalk of rye, among them one not larger than a man's thumb, bearing a straw upon his shoulders.

"Why do you puff so hard?" said the farmer from his hiding-place, "your burden is not so great."

"His burden is according to his strength, for he is but one night old," answered one of the Tomts, "but hereafter you shall have less."

From that day all luck disappeared from the farmer's house, and finally he was reduced to beggary.

* * *

In many districts it has been the custom to set out a bowl of mush for the fairies on Christmas eve.

In the parish of Nyhil there are two estates lying near each other, and both called Tobo. On one was a Tomt, who, on Christmas eve, was usually entertained with wheaten mush and honey. One time the mush was so warm when it was set out that the honey melted. When the Tomt came to the place and failed to find his honey as heretofore, he became so angry that he went to the stable and choked one of the cows to death. After having done this he returned and ate the mush, and, upon emptying the dish, found the honey in the bottom. Repenting his deed of a few minutes before, he carried the dead cow to a neighboring farm and led therefrom a similar cow with which to replace the one he had killed. During his absence the women had been to the barn and returned to the house, where the loss was reported to the men, but when the latter arrived at the cow-shed the missing cow had apparently returned. The next day they heard of the dead cow on the adjoining farm, and understood that the Tomts had been at work.

In one place, in the municipality of Ydre, a housewife remarked that however much she took of meal from the bins there seemed to be no diminution of the store, but rather an augmentation. One day when she went to the larder she espied, through the chinks of the door, a little man sifting meal with all his might.

Noticing that his clothes were very much worn, she thought to reward him for his labor and the good he had brought her, and made him a new suit, which she hung upon the meal bin, hiding herself to see what he would think of his new clothes. When the Tomt came again he noticed the new garments, and at once exchanged his tattered ones for the better, but when he began to sift and found that the meal made his fine clothes dusty he threw the sieve into the corner and said:

"Junker Grand is dusting himself. He shall sift no more."

Herman Hofberg

The Cat of Norrhult*

On the estate of Norrhult, in the parish of Rumskulla, the people in olden times were very much troubled by Trolls and ghosts. The disturbances finally became so unbearable that they were compelled to desert house and home, and seek an asylum with their neighbors. One old man was left behind, and he, because he was so feeble that he could not move with the rest.

Some time thereafter, there came one evening a man having with him a bear, and asked for lodgings for himself and companion. The old man consented, but expressed doubts about his guest being able to endure the disturbances that were likely to occur during the night.

The stranger replied that he was not afraid of noises, and laid himself down, with his bear, near the old man's bed.

Only a few hours had passed, when a multitude of Trolls came into the hut and began their usual clatter. Some of them built the fire in the fireplace, others set the kettle upon the fire, and others again put into the kettle a mess of filth, such as lizards, frogs, worms, etc.

When the mess was cooked, the table was laid and the Trolls sat down to the repast. One of them threw a worm to the bear, and said:

"Will you have a fish, Kitty?"

Another went to the bear keeper and asked him if he would not have some of their food. At this the latter let loose the bear, which struck about him so lustily that soon the whole swarm was flying through the door.

Some time after, the door was again opened, and a Troll with mouth so large that it filled the whole opening peeked in. "Sic him!" said the bear keeper, and the bear soon hunted him away also.

In the morning the stranger gathered the people of the village around him and directed them to raise a cross upon the es-

* Not longer than thirty years ago a cross, said to be the one raised on this occasion, was still standing in Norrhult.

tate, and to engrave a prayer on Cross Mountain, where the Trolls dwelt, and they would be freed from their troublesome visitors.

Seven years later a resident of Norrhult went to Norrköping. On his way home he met a man who asked him where he came from, and, upon being informed, claimed to be a neighbor, and invited the peasant to ride with him on his black horse. Away they went at a lively trot along the road, the peasant supposed, but in fact high up in the air. When it became quite dark the horse stumbled so that the peasant came near falling off.

"It is well you were able to hold on," said the horseman. "That was the point of the steeple of Linköping's cathedral that the horse stumbled against. Listen!" continued he. "Seven years ago I visited Norrhult. You then had a vicious cat there; is it still alive?"

"Yes, truly, and many more," said the peasant.

After a time the rider checked his horse and bade the peasant dismount. When the latter looked around him he found himself at Cross Mountain, near his home.

Some time later another Troll came to the peasant's cottage and asked if that great savage cat still lived.

"Look out!" said the peasant, "she is lying there on the oven, and has seven young ones, all worse than she."

"Oh!" cried the Troll, and rushed for the door. From that time no Trolls have ever visited Norrhult.

Herman Hofberg

Lady Barbro of Brokind[*]

On the estate of Brokind, in the parish of Vardsnäs, dwelt, in days gone by, a rich and distinguished lady named Barbro, who was so hard-hearted and severe with her dependents that for the least transgression they were bound, their hands behind

---

[*] This story was found, after his death, among the papers of the lecturer, J. Vallman. The estate of Brokind, before it came into the possession of the family of Count Falkenberg, was owned, for about two centuries, by the family of Night and Day. It is probable that the Lady Barbro wrought into this legend is Lady Barbro, Erik's daughter, wife of Senator Mons, Johnson Night and Day, though how she was made to play a part in the narrative is not known, as her body was not impaled in a swamp, but rests peacefully in an elegant grave in the cathedral of Linköping.

Swedish Fairy Tales

their backs, and cast into prison, where, to add to their misery, she caused a table, upon which a bountiful supply of food and drink was placed, to be spread before them, which, of course, bound as they were, they could not reach. Upon complaint being made to her that the prisoners were perishing from hunger and thirst, she would reply, laughingly: "They have both food and drink; if they will not partake of it the fault is theirs, not mine." Thus the prison at Brokind was known far and wide, and the spot where it stood is to this day called Kisthagen, in memory of it.

When Lady Barbro finally died she was buried in the grave with her forefathers, in the cathedral of Linköping, but this was followed by such ghostly disturbances that it became necessary to take her body up, when it was interred in the churchyard of Vardsnäs.

Neither was she at rest here, whereupon, at the suggestion of one of the wiser men of the community, her body was again taken up, and, drawn by a yoke of twin oxen, was conveyed to a swamp, where it was deposited and a pole thrust through both coffin and corpse. Ever after, at nightfall, an unearthly noise was heard in the swamp, and the cry of "Barbro, pole! Barbro, pole!"

The spirit was, for the time being, quieted, but, as with ghosts in all old places, it returned after a time, and often a light is seen in the large, uninhabited building at Brokind.

The Urko of North Wij[*]

From the point where the river Bulsjö empties into Lake Sommen, extending in a northerly direction for about eight miles, bordering the parishes of North Wij and Asby, nearly up to a point called Hornäs, stretches the principal fjord, one of several branching off from the large lake.

Near Vishult, in the first named of these parishes, descending to the lake from the elevation that follows its west shores, is a wall-like precipice, Urberg, which, from the lake, presents an especially magnificent view, as well in its height and length, and in its wood-crowned top, as in the wild confusion of rocks at its base, where, among the jumble of piled-up slabs of stones, gape large openings, into which only the imagination dares to intrude.

From this point the mountain range extends southward toward Tulleram, and northward, along the shore of Lake Sjöhult, under the name of Tjorgaberg, until it ends in an agglomeration of rocks called Knut's Den.

In this mountain dwells the Urko, a monster cow of traditionary massiveness, which, in former times, when she was yet loose, plowed the earth, making what is now Lake Sommen and its many fjords. At last she was captured and fettered by a Troll man from Tulleram, who squeezed a horseshoe around the furious animal's neck and confined her in Urberg. For food she has before her a large cow-hide from which she may eat a hair each Christmas eve, but when all the hairs are consumed, she will be liberated and the destruction of Ydre and all the world is to follow.

But even before this she will be liberated from her prison if Ydre is crossed by a king whom she follows and kills if she can catch him before he has crossed to the confines of the territory.

It happened one time that a king named Frode, or Fluga, passed through Ydre, and, conscious of the danger, hurried to

---

[*] This legend doubtless grew out of the story of the flood, in this form relating how the mighty waters burst their bounds and were in time again imprisoned in their beds.

reach the boundaries, but, believing he had already passed them, he halted on the confines at Fruhammer, or, as the place was formerly called, Flude, or Flugehammer, where he was overtaken and gored to death by the monster. In confirmation of this incident, his grave, marked by four stones, is to this day pointed out.

Another narrative, which, however, is known only in the southeastern part of the territory, relates that another king, unconscious of the danger accompanying travel in the neighborhood, passed unharmed over the border, and had reached the estate of Kalleberg, when he heard behind him the dreadful bellowing of the monster in full chase after him. The king hastened away as speedily as possible. The cow monster, unable to check its mad gallop at the border, rushed over some distance to the place where the king first paused, where, in the gravel-mixed field, she pawed up a round hole of several hundred feet in breadth, which became a bog, whose border, especially upon the north side, is surrounded by a broad wall of the upheaved earth.

Still, at times, especially preceding a storm, the Urko is heard rattling its fetters in the mountain, and both upon the mountain and down near the shore of the lake by times.

Extraordinary things are said to happen. One and another of the residents thereabouts assert even that they have seen the Urko in her magnificent rooms and halls, which the neighbors do not for a moment doubt.

Herman Hofberg

The Troll Shoes

Near Koleförs, in the jurisdiction of Kinda, lived, a long time ago, an old woman, who, as the saying goes, was accustomed, during Easter week, to go to Blåkulla.

Late one Passion Wednesday evening, as was usual with witches, she lashed her pack in readiness for the night, to follow her comrades in their wanderings. In order that the start should be accompanied by as few hindrances as possible, she had greased her shoes and stood them by the fireplace to dry.

In the dusk of the evening there came to her hut another old woman, tired and wet through from the rain, and asked permission to remain over night. To this the witch would not consent, but agreed to allow the woman to remain until she had dried her soggy shoes before the fire, while she, unwilling to be under the same roof with her guest, remained outside.

After a time the fire died out, and it became so dark in the hut that when the stranger undertook to find her shoes, in order to continue her journey, she got and put on the witch's shoes instead. Hardly had she passed out through the door when the shoes jerked her legs up into the air and stood her head downward, without, however, lifting her into the air and carrying her away as would have been if the witch's broom had been in her hand.

In this condition the old woman and the shoes struggled through the night. Now the shoes stood her on her head and dragged her along the ground, now the woman succeeded in grasping a bush or root, and was able to regain her feet again for a time.

In the end, near morning, a man walking past, noticed her and hastened to her relief. Answering her earnest pleading the man poked off one of the shoes with a stick, whereupon, instantly, shoe and stick flew into the air and vanished in the twinkling of an eye. After the adventures of the night the old Troll woman was so weakened that she fell into a hole, which is pointed out to this day, and is called "The Troll Woman's Pit."

Herman Hofberg

The Wood and Sea Nymphs*

Both wood nymphs and sea nymphs belong to the giant family, and thus are related.

They often hold communication with each other, although the wood nymphs always hold themselves a little above their cousins, which frequently occasions differences between them.

A peasant, lying in the woods on the shores of Lake Ommeln, heard early one morning voices at the lake side engaged in vehement conversation. Conjecturing that it was the wood nymphs and sea nymphs quarreling, he crept through the underbrush to a spot near where they sat, and listened to the following dialogue:

Sea Nymph — "You shall not say that you are better than I, for I have five golden halls and fifty silver cans in each hall."

Wood Nymph — "I have a mountain which is three miles long and six thousand feet high, and under that mountain is another, ten times higher and formed entirely of bones of the people I have killed."

When the peasant heard this he became so alarmed that he ran a league away, without stopping. Thus he did not learn which was victorious, but it was the wood nymphs without doubt, as they have always been a little superior to the others.

---

* The wood nymph dwells in large forests, and is described as a beautiful young woman, when seen face to face; but if her back be turned to one it is hollow, like a dough-trough, or resembles a block stub. Sometimes, instead of a hollow back, she is adorned with a bushy fox tail. The sea nymph dwells, as indicated by the name, at the bottom of seas and lakes, and is clad in a skirt so snow-white that it sparkles in the sunlight. Over the skirt she wears a light blue jacket. Usually her appearance is the forerunner of a storm; she is then seen sitting upon a billow combing her golden hair.

The Mountain Kitchen*

In the parish of Bolsta there lived, many years ago, a man named Slottbon. One summer evening he rode his horse to pasture up toward Dalo Mountain. Just as he let the horse go, and was turning to go home, a black man confronted him and asked him if he did not wish to see the mountain kitchen.

Slottbon acquiesced and followed his conductor into the mountain, where it seemed to him certain that he must lose his senses among the glitter of gold and silver utensils of the kitchen,

* This legend is noteworthy as being the only one, as far as the author has been able to find, in which Troll property is changed into snakes. Usually gold is changed into shavings, and silver to pebbles and sand; otherwise it brings disaster upon the usurper of Trolldom and his family.

Herman Hofberg

with which he was surrounded.

The mountain man inquired of his guest if he should order something to eat for him, to which Slottbon assented, and, while his host was absent preparing the repast, improved the opportunity to gather up all the gold and silver his leather apron would hold, and with it hasten away with all possible speed, not slacking his pace until he came to a gravel pit, where it occurred to him to look at his treasure. Seating himself upon a stone, he began to throw the vessels, one after the other, upon the ground, where, as fast as they were thrown down, they were turned into serpents.

Thoroughly frightened at the sight, he dropped his whole burden and took to his heels, followed closely by the wriggling mass of enormous reptiles. Finally, when he had about given himself up for lost, he came to and sprang upon the trunk of a fallen tree and cried out, "God save me, poor sinner!" and in the twinkling of an eye the serpents vanished.

Buried Alive[*]

Many years ago an epidemic swept over Dalland, to which thousands of persons fell victims. Many people fled to the forests, or to other regions; the churches were deserted, and those remaining were not enough to bury the dead. At this stage an old Finlander came along, who informed the few survivors that they need not hope for cessation of the scourge until they had buried some living thing.

The advice was followed. First a cock was buried alive, but the plague continued as violent as ever; next, a goat, but this also proved ineffectual. At last a poor boy, who frequented the neighborhood, begging, was lured to a wood-covered hill at the point where the river Daleborg empties into Lake Venem. Here a deep hole was dug, the boy meantime sitting near, enjoying a piece of bread and butter that had been given him. When the grave was deep enough the boy was dropped into it and the diggers began hurriedly to shovel the dirt upon him. The lad begged and prayed them not to throw dirt upon his bread and butter, but the spades flew faster, and in a few minutes, still alive, he was entirely covered and left to his fate.

Whether this stayed the plague is not known, but many who after night pass the hill, hear, it is said, a voice as if from a dying child, crying, "Buried alive! Buried alive!"

---

[*] As late as 1875 a farmer near Mariestad, during an epidemic among his cattle, buried alive a cow in the ground. Whether this cruel expedient was effective the author is not informed.

Herman Hofberg

115

Jonas Spits*

At Helgy, in the parish of Sunne, lived a warrior, by name Jonas Spits, who, in wars against the Russians and others, had gained for himself the reputation of a brave man.

It so happened that there was a revolt in the land, and the king sent a message to Spits, commanding his services in battle. One Sunday morning, after the troops had assembled in the field, Spits

---

* The ennobled Gyllenspits was born at Speserund, in the parish of Millisvik, in Vermland, some time in the year 1609. During the Polish and German wars he made his way up from the ranks to lieutenant-colonel, and was made a noble in 1660. He was afterward colonel, and finally major-general of infantry. He died in 1679, and is buried in Sunne Church, in Vermland.

was engaged in grinding his sword.

"This is right!" said the king. "There will be fighting tomorrow; let me see that you make good use of your weapon then."

"I shall not fail you," answered Spits, and continued his grinding.

The next day brought a bloody conflict, in which Spits' sword was not idle until the evening and the conclusion of the battle, when the king asked for him.

"Here I am," answered Spits, bowing before him.

"Let me see your sword," said the king, "and know what services you have done this day."

"Here it is," said Spits, at the same time reaching for the weapon covered with blood.

"Good!" said the king. "I'll gild this sword for you." Whereupon he knighted him and commanded that he should be called "The Spits of Gyllenspits."

Herman Hofberg

Lady Rangela and Edsholm

A few miles west of Karlstad, on a little island near Slottsbro-sund, was located, in former days, an old fortress called Asa, or Edsholm Castle, otherwise notorious as the residence of the cruel stewards of Vestersysslet.

A niggardly and cruel woman, Lady Rangela, for a time owned Edsholm and all the land thereabout. She soon made herself bitterly hated by the peasantry because of the oppressions she heaped upon them, and especially because of the unreasonable toll she demanded every time they crossed the castle bridge.

According to agreement, two peasants went one day, the one to the top of Edsholm Mountain and the second to a mountain on the other side of the sound near the castle, whereupon the following conversation was carried on between them, in a loud voice:

"My dear neighbor, lend me your large kettle."

"What do you want with it?"

"I want to cook Lady Rangela of Edsholm Castle, because she demands too high toll from passers over the bridge."

"You shall have it gladly."

This was heard at the castle, and Lady Rangela, believing it to be the Trolls planning her destruction, hurriedly packed her treasures and deserted Edsholm. She had, however, gone no further than to Rangelsund, or Ransund, which is named after her, when a severe storm overtook her and sunk the boat, with people, treasure and all.

When the peasantry learned what had happened, they poured into the castle and razed it to the ground, since when there has been nothing to indicate its existence more than a few heaps of gravel.

Saxe of Saxeholm

At the mouth of the Bay of Olme, upon a little island, which on its west side is connected with the island of Kumel, is situated the castle of Saxeholm.

Here dwelt, in former days, a powerful chief, by name Saxe, the greater part of whose time was spent in bloody warfare, in which occupation he seemed to find great success and pleasure. At home he was gloomy and reserved, and very cruel to his wife.

Finally, becoming wearied by her husband's continued harshness, she determined to elope with another who better understood how to reward her love.

One time when Saxe was at Christmas matins in the church at Varnum, his wife set fire to the castle, shut the gates and threw the key over the wall into the garden outside. Preceding this she had commanded that her horses be shod with shoes reversed, thus hoping to bewilder her pursuers, then, with her lover and a few trusty servants, the castle was deserted, and her way taken over the ice-covered bay.

When Saxe came home, he found his castle wrapped in flames, and the following lines written on the outer gate:

"Within is burning Saxe's knout,
And Saxe the cruel must lie without."

What the chiefs thoughts were at such a greeting is not related. Meantime his wife, before she left the castle, had deposited, in one of the vaults, a chest filled with valuables, and had declared that no human power should move it therefrom.

Many attempts have since been made to unearth this treasure, and it is said that more than once the searchers have so far succeeded as to get a glimpse of the iron-bound chest, but always at this point they have been frightened away by an awful voice calling out from the depths of the vault, "Don't come here!"

Herman Hofberg

The Polite Coal Burner[*]

At Vejefors forge, up near the northern frontier, there was, many years ago, a charcoal burner who, however vigilant he might be, always had to rebuild and burn his stacks. Now, the wood was not burned enough, again, poorly burned, and a thousand annoyances pursued him in his work.

One evening, as he sat in his hut mending his tools, a beautiful maiden entered, and, complaining that she was almost frozen, asked permission to warm herself at the fire.

---

[*] From Norway we have a similar story, by Faye, *Norske Folkesagn*, which relates that a wood nymph one time attended a dance, where she had as partner a young man, who, when he observed the bushy appendage, said genteelly, "My beautiful lady, you are losing your garter," which so pleased the nymph that she rewarded him bountifully with gold and other riches

The coal burner, who had been long in the woods, understood at once that his visitor was a wood nymph, beautiful and enchanting when seen face to face, but, when seen behind, is adorned with a bushy fox tail.

"When she had warmed herself in front awhile, she turned her back to the fire, and the coal burner was given an opportunity to see the tail, whereupon, with unexpected courtesy, he addressed his guest;

"Miss, look out for your train, please!"

That nice name for her troublesome appendage won the Troll woman's affections, and from that day everything went admirably with the coal burner.

Herman Hofberg

The Harvesters

In the parish of Ekshärad lies a mountain, Säljeberg, which was formerly the dwelling place of Trolls and Giants, now exterminated.

Near the mountain dwelt a farmer, on one of the best farms in the parish. One summer evening he went over his fields admiring the seas of golden grain and exulting at the abundant harvest promised him.

"God be praised for this crop," said he. "If I now could have all these fields harvested by early morning I would give my best cow."

Hereupon he returned to his home and went to bed. Through the whole night the noise of reaping was heard in the fields and the Trolls calling:

"Make bands and bind; let the farmer dry it himself."

As soon as sunrise the farmer was upon his feet and out into the fields, where, to his indescribable amazement, he saw them reaped and the grain lying in bundles upon the ground. Guessing that the Trolls had had a hand in the work, he sprang to the stable, there to find a stall empty and his best cow gone.

The Ulfgryt Stones

In the peak of Mount Garphytte, one of the many mountain tops that raise themselves over Kilseberger, dwelt, in former days, a giant named Rise.

One morning, as he went from his grotto out into the day, a strange sound, which caused him to pause, greeted his ear. He listened for some time, then returned into the mountain and called his wife.

"Put the smallest of those stones that lie upon the peak into your garter and sling it at that gray cow that goes tinkling along down there by Hjelmaren!" said he, meaning the new church just completed at Orebro, whose bells were that morning ringing for the first time in the service of the Lord.

The giantess, as she was commanded, took a stone as large as a house and threw it at the church, some eight or ten miles distant.

"That was a poor throw," said the giant, when the stone fell down on the plain of Rumbo. "Bring here the band; you shall see a throw that will do its work," whereupon he adjusted a monstrous stone in his wife's garter, and, swinging it a few times through the air, let it go with all his power toward the new church.

"Great in command, but little in power," said the giant woman, when the stone fell upon the one she had thrown, and was broken into a thousand pieces.

At the same time the bell rung out with wonderful clearness. Furious with rage, he tore up two large stones, took one under each arm, and set out for Orebro. Intelligence having reached the residents of Orebro that the giant was coming, consternation was general and good advice dear.

Finally, an old man undertook to save the church. In great haste he gathered up all the worn-out shoes he could find, put them in a sack, and set out to meet the giant. At Ulfgryt, in Toby, he met the giant, who was anything but gentle in appearance.

"How far is it to Orebro?" asked Rise.

"I can't say exactly," answered the old man, in an innocent manner, "but it is long a way, you will find, for it is seven years since I left there, and I have worn out all these shoes on the way."

"Then let him who will, go there, but I will not," said the giant, and threw the stones from him to the ground with such force that they rang as they struck it.

The stones lie there by the roadside even to-day, but the most remarkable circumstance is that they turn over whenever the church bells in Orebro are rung.

Rugga Bridge*

In the last years of the fourteenth century there lived in Strengnäs, the well-known bishop, Konrad Rugga, or Bishop Cort, as he was called by the people. Holding his office at a time when the glory of Papacy was at its height, it is natural that his power was great and influence unusual. Yet tradition has not been content with this, but has magnified his endowments to the almost supernatural.

In order to maintain discipline and order in his bishopric he was wont to travel from place to place in his diocese, always visiting in these journeys the convent of Riseberga.

During one of these official tours he purchased in Tangerosa, three small farms, and made of them a large domain, which he improved and called Trystorp — three farms—but from Riseberga to Trystorp it is a long distance, and as the Bishop was not unskilled in constructing underground ways—he having already completed one such under the Mälar from Strengnäs to his residence, Tynnelsö—he tunneled a passage from the monastery to Trystorp under Logsjö. For the public he built a road above ground, which is the same that now leads to Trystorp around the north shore of Logsjö.

Over a stream, or at that time a little river, which, just below Riseberga, runs from the south in a northerly course, he built a substantial bridge of sandstone. The bridge is even to-day called Rugga's bridge or more commonly Ruggebro.

Not long after the death of Bishop Cort the Papal power was forced to yield in Sweden to the doctrines of Luther and Riseberga to share the fate of other convents in the land.

* Bishop Konrad Rugga, who plays a part in this story, belonged to the old Kyle family and was born in Stockholm. After he had studied in foreign high schools, he was, upon his return to Sweden, first canon, and later archdeacon in Upsala Cathedral. In the year 1480 he was chosen bishop of Strengnäs, which office he entered upon on the 3rd of April, 1501. In the Cathedral of Strengnäs, even now, a small cell is shown, which is said to have been his treasure vault, and where his prayer-book, shoes and other relics may still be seen.

Herman Hofberg

It was now determined to move one of the bells of the convent to Edsberg, where it was to call the people together to hear the new message of truth. But the Bishop's powerful spirit seemed even now to be present on earth, for when they who bore the bell reached the middle of Ruggebro, the burden was overthrown by an unseen hand into the creek, where it disappeared.

Many have since seen the bell, and one and another have even succeeded in raising it half way out of the water, but it has always escaped and sunk back into the creek bed, scoffing at the weakness of the covetous laborers.

Kate of Ysätter

The inhabitants of Närike have many stories to relate about an apparition, called Kate of Ysätter, that in olden times dwelt in Öster Närike's forests, but chiefly in the swamps of Ysätter, in the parish of Asker.

According to the belief of the old people, she existed through many generations, although she usually made her appearance as a young girl beautifully clad, and possessing a head of hair of extraordinary length. She was often seen by hunters sitting upon a stump, combing her hair which reached to the ground. Those who went to the swamps to wash their clothes sometimes saw her at a little distance also washing garments which were of an unusual whiteness. To ugly old women she was always a terror, and it seemed to be a pleasure to her to mimic them by keeping time with their motions, but whenever she showed herself it was for a few seconds only, and should one turn his eyes from her, however little, she was gone.

In Öster Närike, the routes she took were shown, and many complaints were heard that she trampled the grain down in her constant journeys back and forth. Often, especially in the night time, her awful laugh was heard from her perch on a tree or top of a rock, when she succeeded in alluring some one from his path, caused him to fall with his load, or break his harness. Her laugh was like a magpie's, and caused the blood of one helpless against her pranks to stand still

Others who endeavored to stand well with her she assisted in many instances. "She has gone, the lightning has killed her as the others," say the old people, not yet won over to the skepticism of the present time.

Among those who enjoyed her special favor was a hunter, Bottorpa Lasse. He was such a skillful shot that if only he stepped out upon the porch and called a bird, or drew the picture of an animal upon the wall of the barn, the game he wished was brought within range of his gun.

One time Lasse invited his neighbors to accompany him on a hunt, and, expecting to bag an abundance of game, they were not slow to accept the invitation. They betook themselves in the evening to the woods, where they found shelter in a coal burner's hut, and prepared to begin the hunt early in the morning.

Along in the night Kate entered the hut, and requested the hunters to show her their guns. She first examined those of the hunter's neighbors, but soon returned them, exclaiming, "Fie!" She then took Lasse's gun, blew down the barrel, examined the priming and handed it back exclaiming, "Good, good, my boy!" What this signified was soon manifested, when Lasse secured a fine lot of game and the others did not so much as get a shot.

It is further related of Kate of Ysätter, that at the burning of the clock tower of Asker, in the year 1750, when even the church was in flames and in great danger of destruction, Kate was seen standing on the roof, opposing their progress.

The last time she made her presence known was at a harvest gathering in the fields of Ysätter. The harvesters had ceased labor to eat their luncheon, and when they had eaten themselves into a good humor, engaging in conversation, which turned upon Kate, a young man declared he would like nothing better than to catch her and give her a good whipping for the vexations she had produced in the world. Instantly a terrific crash was heard in an enclosure near by, and the youth received a blow in the face that caused the blood to gush from mouth and nose over the food of the others, changing their butter to blood. It was after this that many thought it wise to say as little and to have as little as possible to do with Kate of Ysätter.

The Elves' Dance

Upon the marshy oak and linden covered island of Sor, when the grass starts forth in the spring, are to be seen, here and there, circles of a deeper green than the surrounding grass, which the people say mark the places where Elves have had their ring dances.

While the provost, Lille Strale, was pastor of the parish church, a servant was sent out late one evening to bring a horse in from a pasture. Plodding along as best he could in the darkness, he had not gone far when it was discovered that he had lost his way, and, turn which way he would, he could not find the sought for meadow.

Exhausted at last by constant walking, he sat down at the foot of an oak to rest himself. Presently strains of lovely music reached his ears, and he saw, quite near, a multitude of little people engaged in a lively ring dance upon the sward. So light were their footsteps that the tops of the grass blades were scarcely moved.

In the middle of the ring stood the Elf Queen herself, taller and more beautiful than the others, with a golden crown upon her head and her clothes sparkling in the moonlight with gold and precious stones.

Beckoning to him, she said: "Come, Anders, and tread a dance with me!" and Anders, thinking it would be impolite not to comply with the request of a woman so beautiful, rose and stepped bowing into the ring.

Poor lad, he did not know what a fate awaited him who ventured to participate in the sports of the Elves. How the dance terminated is not known, but at its conclusion the young man found himself again under the oak, and from that hour he was never again wholly himself. From being the most lively and cheerful young man in the village, he became the dullest and most melancholy, and, before the year had gone, his days were ended.

Herman Hofberg

The Fiddler and the Sea Nymph

Many years ago a dancing society of Brästa, a village in the parish of Stora Mellösa, planned a great Christmas festival, to which, on the appointed day, old and young flocked from far and near, knowing that Sexton Kant, of Norrbyås, would be there with his fiddle, and assured that fun would run riot. Kant, it is related, was no ordinary fiddler, not a little proud of his skill, and ready at the least word of praise to laud himself to the skies.

When the merry making had gone well into the night and the pleasures were at their height, some one remarked that not many could measure themselves with Father Kant, when he let the bow leap over the strings and played in "four voices," as he himself called it. Nothing further was needed. Kant, always ready to begin where the others left off, declared that the devil, good player as he was reputed to be, could not compete with him in the waltz which they had just heard. This boast came near costing Kant dear. When the dance ended and he set out in the night on his way home, he met, near the hill of Bjurbäcka, a young woman clad in white, who saluted him and addressed him as follows:

"If you will play a polka for me, Father Kant, I will dance for you."

So said, so done. Father Kant sat himself upon a stone and applied the bow to the strings of the instrument. Instantly he lost all control of himself. Such a polka as now came from his fiddle he had never expected to hear, much less play. The tones seemed to come without help from him. The bow bounded over the strings and his arm was forced to follow. One melody followed another; his arm became numb, but the music continued in the same wild measure.

Kant now understood that something was wrong. Finally he burst forth:

"God forgive me, poor sinner. What have I brought upon myself?"

Upon the instant the fiddle strings parted, and an awful-sounding laugh was heard from the brook at the foot of the hill.

Heavy of heart, Kant hastened homeward, acknowledging to himself that the devil, after all, was his superior. For a long time he could not be persuaded to again take up his fiddle, but, when he finally complied, he found that one of the beautiful waltzes he had played on the eventful night had fastened itself upon his memory, and he acquired greater renown than before as a fiddler.

Herman Hofberg

The Snipe

The snipe, as is well known, is a bird which inhabits low, marshy meadows, and which, in flight, makes a noise with its wings not unlike the neighing of a horse.

A farmer, who himself never looked after his property, had in his employ a lazy and negligent servant. One dry summer the man rode his master's horse, many days in succession, to a pasture where there was no water, without first giving it drink, as he had been instructed. So the poor animal was thus left to suffer through the long dry period.

It happened one day that the farmer would go to the city, and commanded the servant to fetch the horse from the pasture. The man went, but search where he would, no horse could be found. The servant not returning in season, his master set out after him, but neither could he find the animal. It had disappeared from the pasture completely, and was not found again.

Some days later, when the farmer was again out, continuing the search, to his surprise he heard a neighing in the air. Soon after he observed his horse, as he supposed, standing and drinking in an adjoining meadow. "Are you there, Grålle?" cried the farmer, and hastened to catch the horse. His shout was answered with a neigh.

"Grålle, Grålle, my boy!" continued the farmer, in persuasive tones and was about to grasp the halter, when the horse was transformed into a bird, which, with another neigh, flew into the air.

From that day the farmer took care of his own horses, and before all else he saw to it that they did not want for water when they went to pasture.

Herman Hofberg

Tibble Castle and Klinta Spring

At Tibble, in the parish of Bedelunda, there stood, in former days, so it is said, a castle, of which the most careful search fails to reveal any remnant now.

In the castle dwelt a lady of royal descent, with her young and beautiful daughter. One day there came to it a prince, who was received with great pomp, and it was not long until an ardent love had sprung up between the young people. Knowing that many eyes were upon them, keeping expressions in check, they agreed to meet each other on a certain night at Klinta Spring, situated south of the castle near Klinta Mountain.

Late in the evening, when all its inhabitants were asleep, and it had become quiet in the castle, the young lady crept quietly from her room down to the castle gate, but the porter refused to open it for her. Thinking gold might persuade him, she drew from her hand a ring which she tendered him, but he was not so easily bribed. Then she took a gold chain from her neck, proffering it with the ring; such a temptation the old man could not resist, and quietly allowed her to pass, with the condition that she should return before dawn.

When she arrived at the spring she thought she saw the prince sitting upon a stone near by, and, approaching him, she threw herself into his arms. But, instead of that of her lover, she found herself in the embrace of the Mountain King of Klinta Mountain, who lifted her up and bore her into the mountain. Before reaching the interior of the mountain, however, she succeeded in slipping the crown he wore from the giant's head and hanging it, as she passed, upon the branch of a pine tree so that the prince could see that she had kept her appointment.

When they reached the inside of the mountain, the giant laid the young woman carefully down upon the "star spread" in his chamber, where she fell asleep, after which he went to his mother and told her what a beautiful discovery he had made. Meantime the prince came to the spring. When he failed to find his mistress there he walked around the meadow and came, finally, to the mountain, where his attention was attracted to the crown hanging in the tree. He now understood what had happened, and in anguish drew his sword and pierced his body with it. When the young woman awoke, the giant woman commanded her son to carry her back to the spring. "But," added she, "before you reach there three lives will have been forfeited."

And so it happened. While the giant was carrying the young woman to the spring she breathed her last and was laid by the giant at the side of the prince. Meanwhile the porter, in remorse over his deed, had thrown himself from the tower, and thus ended his days.

The prince and his love were laid upon a golden wagon and conveyed to a beautiful green meadow on an eminence near Gryta and there interred. Even the wagon and sword were buried in the mound, which every spring is surrounded by a hedge of white, blooming bird cherry, but both wagon and sword shall, in time, be dug up, when he who is first to see the latter shall receive his mortal wound therefrom.

The Coal Burner and the Troll

On a point which shoots out into the northwest corner of Lake Rasvalen, in the region of Linde, lived, in days past, a coal burner named Nils. His little garden patch was left to a servant boy to care for, while he dwelt always in the forest, chopping coal-wood during the summer and burning it in the winter. However he toiled, nothing but bad luck was returned to him, and, leading all other subjects, poor Nils was the talk of the village where his home was.

One day when he was constructing a stack of wood for burn-

Swedish Fairy Tales

ing, on the other side of the lake near the dark Harg Mountain, a strange woman came to him and asked him if be needed help in his work.

"Yes, indeed; it would be good to have some assistance," answered Nils, whereupon the woman began to carry logs and wood much faster than Nils could draw with his horse, so that by noon the material was on the ground for a new stack. When evening came she asked Nils what he thought of her day's work, and if she might come again next day.

The coal burner could not well say no, so she returned the following day, and daily thereafter. When the stack was burned she assisted him with the drawing, and never before had Nils had so much nor so good coal as that time.

Thus the woman remained with him in the forest three years, during which time she became the mother of three children, but this did not bother the coal burner, for she took care of them so that he had no trouble from them.

When the fourth year had been entered upon she began to be more presuming, and demanded that he take her home with him and make her his wife. This Nils did not like, but, as she was very useful to him in the coal forest, he was careful not to betray his thoughts, and said he would think over the matter.

One day he went to church, where he had not been for many years, and what he heard there set him to thinking as he had not thought since he was an innocent child. He began to reflect whether he had not made a misstep, and if it might not be a Troll woman who had so willingly lent him her company and help.

Involved in these and similar thoughts, returning to his forest home, he forgot that he had made an agreement with the strange woman when she first entered his service, that always upon his arrival, and before approaching the stack, he would strike three times with an ax against an old pine tree standing a little way from the coal kiln. On he went, when suddenly there burst upon his sight a scene that nearly took his wits from him. As he neared the stack he discovered it in bright flames, and around it stood the mother and her three children drawing the coal. They drew

Herman Hofberg

and slacked so that fire, smoke and sparks filled the air high toward the heavens, but instead of pine branches, ordinarily used for slacking, they had bushy tails, with which, after dipping them in the snow, they beat the fire.

When Nils had contemplated this awhile, he crept stealthily back to the pine whose trunk he made echo by three blows from his ax, so that it was heard far away at Harg Mountain. Thereupon he went forward to the stack as if he had seen nothing, and now every thing was as he was accustomed to see it. The stack burned steadily and well, and the woman went about her duties as usual.

When the woman saw Nils again, she renewed her appeals to be allowed to go to his home with him and become his wife.

"Yes, the matter shall be settled now," said Nils, consolingly, and departed for home, ostensibly to fetch his horse, but he went instead to Kallernäs, on the east shores of the lake, where lived a wise old man, whom he asked what course to pursue to free himself from the dilemma. The old man advised him to go home and hitch his horse to the coal cart, but so harness that no loops should be found in the reins or harness. Then he should ride over the ice on the back of the horse; turn at the coal-kiln without pausing; shout to the Troll woman and children to get into the cart; and drive briskly to the ice again.

The coal burner, following the instructions, harnessed his horse and saw to it carefully that there was no loop upon the reins or harness, rode over the ice, up into the woods to the kiln and called to the woman and her children to jump in, at the same time heading for the ice and putting his horse to the best possible speed. When he reached the middle of the lake, he saw, running toward him from the wilderness, a large pack of wolves, whereupon he let slip the harness from the shafts, so that the cart and its contents were left standing on the slippery ice, and rode as fast as the horse could carry him straight to the other shore. When the Troll saw the wolves she began to call and beg. "Come back! Come back!" she shrieked. "If you will not do it for my sake, do it for your youngest daughter, Vipa!" But Nils continued his way toward the shore. Then he heard the Trolls calling one to the other, "Brother in Harsberg, sister in Stripa, and cousin in Ringshällen, catch hold of the loops and pull!" "He has no loop," came a reply from the depths of Harsberg.

"Catch him at Härkällarn, then."

"He does not ride in that direction," came from Ringshällen, and Nils did not go that way, but over fields, stones and roads straight to his home, where he had only arrived when the horse fell dead, and a Troll shot came and tore away the corner of the stable.

Nils, himself, fell ill shortly after, and was confined to his bed many weeks. When he recovered his health he sold his cabin in the forest, and cultivated the few acres around his cottage until the end of his days. Thus the Trolls were once caught napping.

Herman Hofberg

Bolstre Castle

One evening, a long time ago, a little girl went up through the forest to Bolstre Castle in search of some sheep that had gone astray.

Reaching the inside of the walls the little girl was met by an old woman, clothed in a red skirt and a gray head covering, who gave into her possession a box, and commanded her to take care of it while she went to invite a number of her friends to become guests at her daughter's wedding.

The girl was so frightened that she did not dare to refuse the charge, and, taking the box, sat down upon a stone to wait the woman's return. When she had thus sat a long time she heard a bird twittering over her head in a tree, and looking up, two leaves fell from the tree in such a manner as to form a cross upon the box, whereupon the cover instantly flew open and revealed its contents—a bridal crown of shining gold and many other costly jewels.

The girl waited long and patiently, but the old woman did not return, so, finally she set out on her way home, taking with her the jewel casket. But blessings do not go with Troll property. No bride would wear the crown, it was so fine, and the girl soon after lost her lover. Now that it was clear to every one that a Troll's gold brought only misfortune upon the household, it was carried back to the castle and buried in the ground, where it surely lies today.

Herman Hofberg

143

The Changelings

Every intelligent grandmother knows that the fire must not be allowed to go out in a room, where there is a child not yet christened; that the water in which the new-born child is washed should not be thrown out; also, that a needle, or some other article of steel, must be attached to its bandages. If attention is not paid to these precautions it may happen that the child will be exchanged by the Trolls, as once occurred in Bettna many years ago.

A young peasant's wife had given birth to her first child. Her mother, who lived some distance away, was on hand to officiate in the first duties attending its coming, but the evening before the day on which the child should be christened she was obliged to go home for a short time to attend to the wants of her own family, and during her absence the fire was allowed to go out.

Now one would have noticed anything unusual, perhaps if the child had not, during the baptism, cried like a fiend. After some weeks, however, the parents began to observe a change. It became ugly, cried continuously and was so greedy that it devoured everything that came in its way. The people being poor, they were in great danger of being eaten out of house and home. There could no longer be any doubt that the child was a "changeling." Whereupon the husband sought a wise old woman, who, it was said, could instruct the parents what to do to get back their own child.

The mother was directed to build a fire in the bake oven three Thursday evenings in succession, lay the young one upon the bake shovel, then pretend that she was about to throw it into the fire. The advice was followed, and when the woman, the third evening, was in the act of throwing the changeling into the fire, it seemed, a little deformed, evil-eyed woman rushed up with the natural child, threw it in the crib and requested the return of her child. "For," said she, "I have never treated your child so badly and I have never thought to do it such harm as you now propose doing mine," whereupon she took the unnatural child and vanished through the door.

Another changeling story, but with less unfortunate consequences, is told in Södermanland.

A resident of Vingåkir, who made frequent trips to Nyköping with loads of flour, was in the habit of halting for the night at the house of a farmer in Verna. One summer night he arrived later than usual, and, as the people were already in bed and asleep, the weather being pleasant, he did not wish to wake anyone, so unhitched his horse from the wagon, hitched him to a hay stack and laid himself under the wagon to sleep.

He had been some time under the wagon, yet awake, when, from under a stone near by, an ugly, deformed woman, carrying a babe, made her appearance. Looking about her carefully, she laid the child on the stone and went in the house. In a short time, she returned, bearing another child; laid it upon the stone, and taking up the first one, returned to the house.

The man observed her actions, and divining their purpose, crept cautiously from his resting place as soon as the woman had disappeared into the house, took the sleeping child and hid it in his coat under the wagon. When the troll returned and found the child gone she went a third time to the house, from which she returned with the child she had just carried in, whereupon she disappeared under the stone.

The traveler, anxious for the welfare of his little charge, which had in such an extraordinary manner fallen into his hands, could not close his eyes for the rest of the night.

As soon as it dawned he went with his precious burden to the house, where he found the occupants in great consternation over the disappearance of the child, which, as may be presumed, was received with great rejoicing.

Herman Hofberg

The Lady of Pintorp*

What is now the country seat of Eriksberg, with its castle-like buildings among parks and gardens, was once an estate called Pintorp, upon which tradition has fixed the melancholy story of "The Lady of Pintorp."

At Pintrop, so goes the story, lived a nobleman who, at his death, yet a young man, left his goods and estates to his widow. Instead of proving a good mistress to her numerous dependents, she impoverished them in all possible ways and treated them with the greatest cruelty. Under the castle she had deep cells, the terrors of which, on the slightest provocation, many a poor innocent creature was made to experience. She would set vicious dogs on beggars and children, and he would was not at his work at a fixed hour could be certain that he would go home in the evening with his back well lashed.

Early one morning the Lady of Pintorp stood on the castle steps watching the people congregate for the day's work. Noticing an unfortune fellow a little behind time, she flew into a rage, pouring upon him a flood of abuse and curses, and in punishment commanded him to fell the largest oak to be found upon the estate, and to carry it, before evening, uncut, top foremost, to the garden. If he failed to execute the command fully and punctually

---

* The chief character in this narrative is the wife of President and Senator Erik Gyllerstierna, Beata, to whom the name of Lady Pintorpa is given. As far as can be judged from the best accounts obtainable, Lady Beata was a woman of unusual understanding, decision and power. It is quite possible that in her exactions and treatment of her servants and dependents she may have sometimes been unreasonably severe, and that therefore she did not command their love. It is certain that the stories of her inhuman conduct and tragical end are of a later date than her generation, and that this is a localization of a similar German legend. The opinion is ever hazarded that Beata Yxhull came to play a part in this gruesome myth, alone becamse of the name of the estate, Pintorp, which our uncritical storytellers have credulously taken for granted, was derived from Pina—to tease—though good grounds exist for the belief that the estate took the name from the family of Pinaur, who, in former days, resided theron.

Swedish Fairy Tales

Herman Hofberg

147

he was to be mercilessly driven from the estate and all his possessions confiscated.

Pondering over his sentence the man went to the woods where he met an old man who inquired why he looked so sad.

"Because I am done for, if the Lord does not come to my aid," sighed the unfortunate fellow, and informed the old man what a task his mistress had put upon him.

"Don't be uneasy," said the stranger, "but chop that oak, then set yourself upon the trunk, when Erik Gyllerstierna and Svante Baner will draw it to the castle."

The peasant, as he was instructed, began to cut the tree, which fell with a great crash at the third blow of his ax. Taking his seat upon the trunk, the tree at once began to move as if drawn by horses. The speed was soon so great that opposing fences and gates were brushed aside like straws, and in a short time the oak had arrived at the designated spot in the castle yard. Just as the tree top struck the castle gate one of the invisible haulers stumbled, and a voice was heard to say, "What, you on your knees, Svante?"

The lady who was standing upon the steps at the time understood, without anything further, who had been the laborer's helpers, but instead of repenting she began to swear, scold and in the end, to threaten the man with imprisonment. Hereupon there was an earthquake which shook the walls of the castle, and a black carriage drawn by two black horses stood in the castle yard. A handsome man dressed in black stepped from the carriage, bowed to the lady, and bade her prepare to follow him. Tremblingly—for she knew well who the stranger was—she begged him to let her remain three years yet; to this the visitor would not consent. She begged for three months; this was also denied her, and at last she prayed for three days, then three hours, but was allowed only three minutes in which to dispose of her household affairs.

When she saw that prayers availed her nothing she asked him to, at least, allow her curate, chambermaid and house servants to go with her on the journey. This was granted, so they entered the carriage, which was instantly under way and went off at such a speed that the people who stood in the yard saw nothing but a black streak behind it.

When the lady and her followers had ridden some time they came to a lighted castle, up the steps of which the black gentleman conducted them. Arriving in the hall, he deprived the lady of her rich clothes and gave her instead a coarse gown and wooden shoes. Next he combed her hair three times with such a vengeance that the blood streamed from her head, and concluded by dancing with her three times until her shoes were filled with blood.

After the first dance she asked permission to give her gold ring to her chamberlain, whose fingers were burned by it as with fire. After the second dance she gave the chambermaid her key ring, which scorched her fingers as if glowing iron. At the termination of the third dance a trap in the floor opened and the woman vanished in a cloud of smoke and flame.

The priest who stood nearest peeped with curiosity into the opening where the woman had gone down, when a spark came up from below and hit him in the eye so that thereafter he had but one eye.

When all was over the gentleman in black gave the servants permission to return home, but with strong injunctions not to look back. Hurriedly they sprang into the carriage. The way was broad and straight, and the horses galloped with great speed, but the chambermaid could not control her curiosity, and looked back. Instantly the carriage, horses, even the road disappeared and the travelers found themselves in a wild forest, where they wandered three years before finding their way back to Pintorp.

Herman Hofberg

Lake Goldring[*]

About a mile and a half from Strengnäs lies a narrow valley, between several wood-covered heights and the island upon which in olden times Ingiald Illrada burned herself and all her attendants.

The valley is called Eldsund, and was formerly an open water way connecting two of lake Mälar's bays. Vessels went, then, unhindered through there, and not many years ago a sunken vessel was found, buried in the mud that had one time been at its bottom. Now there is nothing but a small stream winding its way between grass-grown banks, and cows and goats graze where the perch and the pike formerly had their playground.

At one place this little stream spreads its banks until a small lake is formed, which was once of quite respectable size, but is now almost grown over with reeds. Many a poor man has there caught a fish for his pot, that otherwise would have been empty enough.

A good while back there lived a lady on the estate not far from this lake, perhaps as near as Näsbyholm, upon which, near the water-course, lies the notable "cuckoo stone."

This lady was very rich and still more proud, looking with contempt upon all who had less money and lands than she, and were not of as noble blood as she believed herself to be.

One day an old priest visited her. A priest in all respects, not one of those accommodating fellows that could be sent to stir the fire, or one who went with bent back away from home and was painfully straight at home, but a priest who did not hide his thoughts under a chair.

While the priest and his hostess were one day walking along the lake shore, she began, as was her habit, to boast of her riches; to tell how much money she had at interest, and how many tax

* The legend of the ring, originally an Oriental tale [See Herodotus on King Polycrates in Samos], has become a part of the folk-lore of several localities in Scandinavia, as in Närike, The Rich Lady; in Norway, The Insolent Priest's Daughter; in Denmark, Free Birthe, etc.

Swedish Fairy Tales

lists she had complete and incomplete, whereupon the priest asked her how far she thought all that went, or what, after all, it amounted to, for she could not take her riches with her into the grave. At this the lady became angered, and declared that she was so rich that if she should live even many hundreds of years she need not want, and that it was as impossible that she should become poor as it would be to recover her gold ring from the depths of the lake—at the same time drawing a ring from her finger and casting it far out into the water.

The priest maintained that as wonderful things as this had happened in the world, and that it was not more impossible that herring might be recovered than that she might become poor.

Later in the day an old fisherman came to the house with fish to sell. A number were bought, and the kitchen girl was given the task of cleaning them.

When she cut open the largest pike, she saw something shining, and, upon looking with greater care, she recognized her mistress' most valuable finger ring. In great haste she rushed to the lady, who sat wrangling with the moderate priest because he could think it possible her riches might be taken from her.

"Has my lady lost her ring?" asked the maid.

The lady ceased to talk, and cast a glance at the priest, who sat quietly at the window looking out toward the lake.

"Here it is, any way," said the maid, and laid the ring upon the table.

The lady grew pale, but the priest looked more serious than ever.

How it went with her and her riches thereafter, the story does not relate, but the lake is called Goldring to this day.

Herman Hofberg

The Trolls' Garden at Stallsbacke

In the forest north of Stora Djulo, in the parish of Stora Malm, lies a hill called Stallsbacke—Stall Hill— because King Charles XI is said to have had his stable there on one of his journeys.

Within the forest near the hill there is an enchanted garden where many a man has gone astray, and has been compelled to wander the whole night through, because he did not know that turning his coat inside out, or throwing fire at the sun, would give him the key to his deliverance.

Many have, during these wanderings, been imprisoned in the enchanted garden, but not all have liberated themselves from the enchantment as old Lofberg, the steward from Stora Djulo, succeeded in doing.

Late one Thursday evening, while traveling the path from the pasture home to the mansion, he found himself suddenly in the presence of a high wall with grated gates, beyond which was visible the most beautiful garden ever seen by man. The moon was high in the heavens, and Lofberg could distinguish objects as clearly as in daylight. He saw that the trees hung full of fruit, and that the bushes were bowed with berries, which glistened like precious stones. When he had viewed the magnificent sight a few minutes, and was about to go on, an old man, who proclaimed himself the gardener, presented himself, and invited Lofberg to go in and gather of the fruit what he pleased. But Lofberg was too wise for this. He understod that what he saw was the work of the Trolls, and answered that at home there was a much more beautiful garden, and that he had no occasion to go into strange gardens to get a few rotten, sour apples.

This he should not have said. Suddenly there came up a strong wind, which blew his hat over the wall, and, as Lofberg left it behind him and hastened home, there came a crash in the forest, whereupon the vision suddenly melted away.

Herman Hofberg

Herr Melker of Veckholm[*]

In the parish of Veckholm, east of Svingarn Fjord, lived, in the fifteenth century, a priest widely known for his wisdom and goodness. No day went by that he did not read his Bible, and in the evening, when others had gone to rest, he went to the church to offer up his prayers at the altar.

[*] Supplementing this story, it is related that the punishment meted out to the priest's worldly-minded wife for seducing the servant into the attempt to frighten her husband from his devotions was that her body after death should remain in the grave undecayed. The same story is told of a woman member of the old family of Ickorna, and the attempt has been made to establish that she is identical with the woman of Veckholm.

His wife, who attended only to her worldly affairs, and did not look upon these nightly ramblings kindly, determined to put an end to them, and to this end, one evening, called into service one of the servants. "Lasse," said she, "if you will put a white sheet over you and stand in the dark near the path and frighten father when he comes from the church, you shall have a pot of ale."

The man had nothing against this, and with the assistance of his mistress, clad himself as directed and took a position near the path connecting the church and parsonage.

After awhile the priest came from the church. Upon observing the spook, he read a prayer and bade the apparition sink into the ground.

The man sank into the ground to his knees without betraying himself, but continued to play the ghost. The priest prayed again, when Lasse sank into the ground to his waist.

"It is I! Dear father! It is I!" cried Lasse, now in consternation.

"It is too late! Too late, Lasse!" replied the priest, with a sorrowful voice. At the same time the servant sank alive into the earth out of sight.

To commemorate the incident, a wooden cross was raised on the spot, which is always replaced by a new one when the old one has become old and decayed.

Herman Hofberg

The Old Man of Lagga

Near Lagga Church, in the municipality of Langhundra, is a singularly formed mountain. On the side of it toward the church is an opening, from which, it is said, two paths lead—the one south to a hill near the so called "Meadow Watcher's Cottage," the other north to Kashögen, near Kasby estate.

In the mountain lived a giant called Lagge Gubben—old man Lagge—who, when last seen, was at least five hundred years old, and his hair as white as the feathers of a dove.

Early one morning a peasant named Jacob going to the village of Lagga, passed the mountain, when the old mountain man came out and saluted him: "Good morning, Joppe! Will you come in and drink healths with me?"

"No, thank you," replied Jacob, who had no desire for such companionship. "If you have more than you are able to drink, save it until morning, for there is another day coming."

"That is good advice," said Lagga. "Had I known that before, I should have been a richer man, now."

"It is not yet too late," replied the peasant.

"Yes it is, for I must leave here in the morning on account of the church bells," said the giant, shaking his fist at Lagga clock tower.

"You will come again, never fear," said Jacob consolingly.

"Yes, when Lagga Fjord becomes a field and Ostund Lake a meadow," replied the giant with a sigh, and disappeared into the mountain.

The Water Nymph[*]

About a mile northwest from Järna Church was located, at one time, a water mill, Snöåqvarn, belonging to the parishoners of Näs.

One Sunday morning, before the church of Järna had a priest of its own, the chaplain of Näs set out for that place, and had just arrived at the mill, when he saw a water man sitting in the rapids below it, playing on a fiddle a psalm from a psalm book.

"What good do you think your playing will do you?" said the priest. "You need expect no mercy!"

Sadly the figure ceased playing, and broke his fiddle in pieces, whereupon the priest regretted his severe condemnation, and again spoke:

"God knows, maybe, after all."

"Is that so?" exclaimed the man in joy, "then I'll pick up my pieces and play better and more charmingly than before."

To another mill in the same parish, Lindqvarn, near Lindsnäs, a peasant came one time with his grist. Along in the night he thought he would go and see if it was yet ground. He noticed on his arrival that the mill was not running, and opened the wicket to the wheel-house to learn what the matter might be, when he saw, glaring at him from the water below, two eyes as large as half moons.

"The devil! What great eyes you have!" cried the peasant, but received no reply.

"Whew! What monstrous eyes you have!" the peasant again cried; again no answer.

Then he sprang into the mill, where he stirred up a large fire

---

[*] The water nymphs are noted musicians; their music usually being in a plaintive strain and expressing a longing to be released on the day of judgment. Sometimes, but not so often, they appear in the folk-lore as the capricious rulers of the streams which they inhabit. It is believed, in certain regions, that one should not grind grain on the night before Christmas, for at that time the nymphs are out in all the streams, and if they find a mill going they stop it, break it, or grind at such a furious rate that the millstones burst.

Herman Hofberg

brand, with which he returned.

"Are your eyes as large now?" he shouted through the wicket.

"Yes!" came in answer from the stream.

Hereupon the peasant ran the stick through a hole in the floor, where the voice seemed to come from, and at once the wheel began to turn again.

Bölsbjörn[*]

Many generations ago there lived at Bole, in the parish of Ore, a man named Bölsbjörn, noted far and wide for his wonderful strength.

The king, hearing about him, commanded him to come to Stockholm and wrestle with a newly arrived foreign champion named Stenbock, who was said to be so strong that he had never found his superior.

Bölsbjörn hastened to obey the king's command. Strapping his skates upon him, he set off at such a speed that his dog, which had followed him, gave out and died on the way, and the new-baked bread put into his haversack was yet warm upon his arrival at Stockholm.

He was conducted to the king, and was told that he might name his own reward, however great it might be, if he would vanquish Stenbock.

The struggle was soon begun and suddenly concluded by Bölsbjörn laying his antagonist upon his back with such force that three of his ribs were broken. For his reward, Bölsbjörn demanded as much land as he could skate around in one day, and it was granted him by the king.

When he returned home he had made the circuit of nearly twelve square miles of land, which his descendants to this day occupy.

---

[*] It is believed this comes from an old Icelandic Saga, which has been made a part of the folk-lore of Dalarne.

Herman Hofberg

The Treasure Seekers

It is an established rule that he who seeks buried treasures must carefully maintain the utmost silence, lest his search be in vain and harm befall him, body and soul.

They were not ignorant of this—the four men that one time made up a party for the purpose of unearthing treasures said to be buried in Josäterdal.

Making their way, one midsummer night, across Lake Sälen, they saw approaching them a man of strange aspect, behind whose boat dragged a large fir tree, and a little later another, who inquired if they had seen any float-wood on their way.

The treasure seekers, who understood that these rowers were no other than fairies, pretended not to hear the question, and reached Josäterdal finally, without further temptation.

Just as they began to dig in the hill a grand officer approached and addressed them, but no one answered. Soon after a number of soldiers marched up and began to shoot at the diggers, but they did not allow even this to disturb them. Suddenly a red calf hopped up and the soldiers pressed nearer, so that the men soon stood enveloped in powder-smoke so thick that they could not see each other. When this did not frighten them, a tall gallows was raised on the side of the hill. It so happened that one of the diggers wore a red shirt that attracted the attention of the spirits, one of which cried out:

"Shall we begin with him wearing the red shirt?" Whereupon he lost his courage and took to his heels, followed neck over head by the others.

The Lapp in Magpie Form[*]

A Finn in the forests of Safsen, having for a long time suffered ill luck with his flock, determined, let the cost be what it would, to find, through a Lapp well versed in the arts of the Trolls, a remedy for the evil he was enduring.

To this end he set out for the home of his to-be-deliverer, and after a long and fatiguing journey through the wilderness, he came at last to a Lapp hut which, with no little quaking, he entered, and there found a man busied with a fire upon the floor.

* The magpie in folk-lore is an ominous bird, and is avoided by the peasantry, because one cannot know whether it is the spirit of a Troll, friend or foe. When the magpies build near the house it is regarded as a lucky omen, but if they build on the heath, and meantime come to the house and chatter, it bodes evil.

Herman Hofberg

The Lapp who, through his connection with the Trolls, already knew the purpose of the visit, and very much flattered thereby, greeted his guest kindly, and said:

"Good morning, Juga, my boy, are you here? I can give you news from home. Everything goes well there. I was there yesterday."

The Finn was terribly frightened at the discovery that he was recognized, but now more when he heard that the Lapp had made the same journey forth and back in one day, that had cost him so many days of wandering.

With assurance of friendship, the Lapp quieted his fears, and continued:

"I had a little matter to attend to yesterday at your home, and sat upon the housetop when your wife went over the garden, but I saw she did not know me, for she threatened me with the house key."

The Finn now made known his errand, and received for answer that his animals were even now doing as well as he could wish. The presents brought by the Finn greatly strengthened their pleasant relations, and the Lapp agreed willingly to initiate him into the mysteries of Trolldom.

When the Finn reached home, the incidents of his journey were circumstantially related to his wife, even to the Lapp's account of his visit, and the threats with the house key.

"Yes, I remember now," said she, "that a magpie sat upon the roof the same day that the animals seemed to revive, but I believed it to be an unlucky bird, therefore tried to frighten it away with the key."

The Finn and his wife now understood that it was their friend, who had transformed himself thus in order to do them a service, and from that time held these creatures in great veneration.

The Plague*

Memories of the epidemics that have ravaged our country still live in the minds of the people, though, with time, like many other recollections, they have taken the form of myths.

During the plague there was seen, wandering from village to village, a boy and a girl, the one with a rake, the other with a broom. Wherever the boy was seen to use his rake, one and another was spared from death, but where the girl swept, death left an empty house, and the places that were not approached by these beings escaped the plague entirely.

On Soller Island, in Siljan, they strewed gold and precious stones along the roads and paths, which were so infected that he who so much as moved one with his hand became a corpse before the next sunset. In the end there remained no one on the island except two wise old men, one named Bengh, the other Harold, who were not deluded by the gold, thereby saving their lives.

A number of the islanders escaped by flight and moved to the North Land through the "Twelve-Mile Roads" that bordered upon Vermland.

Among those who fled was a young and beautiful maiden named Malin, who, when she came out upon the road, observed a glittering jewel, which, upon closer inspection, represented Christ upon the cross. Notwithstanding the warning of her companions, she could not resist the temptation to pick up the doubly valuable article.

When they came later to their first camping place, Rossberg, about four miles from Soller Island, Malin was seen to fall upon her knees and give herself up to earnest prayer, but just as the evening sun hid himself behind a mountain, she sank lifeless upon a stone, which even to this day is called "Malin's Church," and is dressed every midsummer by the herdsmen with fresh leaves and fragrant flowers.

---

* In other regions it is related that heralding an epidemic, a little bird flies around the country where men are plowing, and, perched upon the ox-yokes, twitters its warning.

Herman Hofberg

The Vätters*

Vätters, according to the Northern belief, are creatures that live under ground, but often appear above, and then in human form so perfect that they have many times been mistaken for mankind. They live, as do the Trolls and Giants, in mountains, but more often move from one to another, and it is mostly during these journeys that they are seen.

When the parish of Ockilbo was first settled, the Vätters were so plentiful that a peasant who fixed his abode near the Rönn Hills was forced to build his windows high up near the eaves of his cottage to escape seeing the troublesome multitude of these beings that continually swarmed around.

Despite the disposition of the cottager to have nothing to do with the Vätters, he could not avoid getting into complications with them at times.

One evening, when the wife went to drive the goats into the goat house, she saw among hers two strange goats, having horse-hoofs instead of cloven hoofs, as should be. Do her utmost, it was impossible to separate them from the others. They pressed on, and were locked up with the rest.

In the night she was awakened by a heavy pounding upon the walls, and a voice from without called:

"Let us be neighborly, mother, and return my goats to me."

The woman dressed herself and hastened to the goat house, where the strange animals were making a dreadful uproar. Upon her opening the door they sprang out and hurried to the forest, whence she heard the Vätters shouting and calling them.

---

* To the characteristics attributed in this story to the Vätters may be added that they are peaceable and generally inclined to be friendly to mankind, but that they may, nevertheless, be aroused to acts of violence if their wishes are not heeded, or if harm is done them designedly. They are said to have great quantities of gold and silver, but steel is very offensive to them. If, therefore, a knife is stuck into a fissure in a mountain, a piece of gold will, a few days later, be found in its stead. During autumn and in winter they take up their abode in vacated cow barns, where they employ themselves after the manner of mankind.

Thus a friendly feeling was forever established between the cottager and the Vätters, and from that day there were no more disturbances.

Herman Hofberg

Forssa Church

In the village Tåsta—Tattestad — in the parish of Hög, lived in former times a widely renowned man named Tatte, whose son, Blacke, after whom the high mountain, Blackåsberg, was named, dwelt in Nannestad, a village in the parish of Forssa.

When the father and son were baptized they together built the church of Hog, in commemoration of the event. Upon its completion Blacke, whose home was a long ride distant, stipulated that the bells, calling the people to worship, should never be rung until his white horse was seen on Åsaks Hill.

One Christmas day, when Blacke was later than usual, Tatte commanded that the bell be rung, and the services had already begun when Blacke arrived at the church. In anger he tore the runic engraved ring from the church door, with prayers bound it upon his horse, made a vow that he would build a church of his own where the ring fell to the ground, and mounting his horse, rode away at full speed.

While crossing Lake Forssa the ice broke, and the horse was plunged into the water, but both horse and rider, however, succeeded in reaching the shore, where the horse shook himself so violently that the ring was loosened and fell to the earth. Blacke kept his word and built a church, which, after the adjacent lake, was called Forssa Church.

Swedish Fairy Tales

Starkad and Bale

The renowned hero, Starkad, the greatest warrior of the North, had offended a princess, therefore had fallen under the displeasure of the king, to escape whose wrath he wandered northward, where he took up his abode at Rude in Tuna, and it is related in the folk stories that he then took the name of "Ala Dräng," or "Rödu Pilt."

In Balbo, nine miles distant, in the parish of Borgajö, dwelt another warrior, Bale, who was a good friend to Starkad, and a companion in arms.

One morning Starkad climbed to the top of Klefberg, in Tuna, and addressed Bale, thus: "Bale in Balbo, are you awake?"

"Rödu Pilt," answered Bale, nine miles away, "the sun and I always awake at the same time; but how is it with you?"

"Poorly enough! I have only salmon for breakfast, dinner and supper. Bring me a piece of meat."

"All right!" replied Bale, and in a few hours arrived in Tuna with an elk under each arm.

The following morning Bale stood upon a mountain in Balbo and shouted: "Rödu Pilt, are you awake?"

"The sun and I awake always at the same time," answered Starkad, "but how is it with you?"

"Oh, I have nothing but meat to eat—elk for breakfast, elk for dinner and elk for supper, come, therefore, and bring me a fish."

"All right," said Starkad, and in a little while he was with his friend, bearing a barrel of salmon under each arm. In this manner the warriors kept each other supplied with fresh game from forest and sea, meantime spreading desolation and terror through the country, but one evening as they were returning from a plundering expedition to the sea, a black cloud appeared, and it began to thunder and lighten. Both hastened on the way, but readied no further than to Vattjom, when Starkad was struck dead by lightning. His companion buried him in a hill around which he placed five stones, two at his feet, one at each shoulder and one at his head, marking to this day the grave of Starkad forty feet in length.

Herman Hofberg

The Bell in Själevad

When the church at Själevad was about to be built, parishioners could not agree upon a location. Those who resided farthest north wished it built at Hemling, and those dwelling to the south desired it more convenient to them. To terminate the wrangle an agreement was arrived at as ingenious as simple. Two logs were thrown out into Höratt Sound, and it was decided that if they floated out to sea the church should be built at Voge, but if they floated in toward the Fjord of Själevad, Hemling should be the building spot.

It happened that just then it was full high tide, when the current changes from its usual course, and in consequence the logs floated in favor of Hemling.

Swedish Fairy Tales

The Southerners found it hard to swallow their disappointment and at once set their wits at work to find a way to defeat the accidental good luck of their neighbors. In the old chapel of Hemling there was an unusually large bell, said to have been brought from some strange land, and regarded with great veneration. Upon this the Southerners set their hope. One beautiful night they stole the bell and took it southward, persuaded that their opponents would follow and build the church near Voge. But the bell, which knew best where the church ought to stand, provided itself with invisible wings and started to fly back to the place from which it had been brought.

As it was winging its way homeward, an old woman standing on Karnigberg—Hag Mountain—saw something strange floating through the air, at which she stared earnestly, wondering what it could be, finally recognizing the much prized bell of the parish, whereupon she cried out:—

"Oh! See our holy church bell!"

Nothing more was needed to deprive the bell of its power of locomotion and it plunged, like a stone, into Prest Sund—priest sound—where, every winter, a hole in the ice marks its resting place at the bottom.

Herman Hofberg

The Vätts' Storehouse

In Herjedalen, as in many of the northern regions of our country, where there is yet something remaining of the primitive pastoral life, there are still kept alive reminiscences of a very ancient people, whose occupation was herding cattle, which constituted their wealth and support. It is, however, with a later and more civilized people, though no date is given, that this narrative deals.

In days gone by, so the story goes, it happened that a milkmaid did not produce as much milk and butter from her herd as usual, for which her master took her severely to task. The girl sought vindication by charging it upon the Vätts, who, she claimed, possessed the place and appropriated a share of the product of the herd. This, the master was not willing to believe, but, to satisfy himself, went one autumn evening, after the cattle had been brought home, to the dairy house, where he secreted himself, as he supposed, under an upturned cheese kettle. He had not sat in his hiding place long when a Vätt mother with her family—a large one—came trooping in and began preparation for their meal.

The mother, who was busy at the fireplace, finally inquired if all had spoons.

"Yes," replied one of the Vätts. "All except him under the kettle."

The dairyman's doubts were now dispelled, and he hastened to move his residence to another place.

Herman Hofberg

The Stone in Grönan Dal

It is probable that the "Stone in Grönan Dal" is like the traditional Phoenix, a pure tradition, since it has never been found by any one of the many who have made pilgrimages to the valley in search of it, for the purpose of deciphering the Runic characters said to be engraved thereon. Yet many stories are widely current in the land concerning it, and the old people relate the following:

When St. Jaffen, "the Apostle of the North," was one time riding through Jämtland from the borders of Norway, his way led along a beautiful green valley, in the parish of Åre. Becoming weary, he dismounted and laid himself down for a nap. When he awoke it occurred to him that such a garden spot must some day be inhabited by mankind, so, selecting a slab of stone, he cut in its surface the following prophetic lines:

Swedish Fairy Tales

When Swedish men adopt foreign customs
And the land loses its old honor,
Yet, shall stand the Stone in Grönan Dal.

When churches are converted into prisons,
And God's services have lost their joyous light,
Yet shall stand the Stone in Grönan Dal.

When rogues and villains thrive
And honest men are banished,
Yet will stand the Stone in Grönan Dal.

When priests become beggars,
And farmers monsters,
Then shall lie the Stone in Grönan Dal.

When the Governor of the Province, Baron Tilas, in 1742, traveled through Jämtland, he found, a few paces east of the gate of Skurdal, a stone lying, which he concluded must be the stone so much talked about. When his coat of arms and the date had been engraved upon it, he caused it to be raised, so that, "even yet it stands, the Stone in Grönan Dal."

Herman Hofberg

The Voyage in a Lapp Sled

In the great forest west of Samsele, a hunter, early one morning, pursued his way in quest of game. About midday he ascended a ridge, where he was overtaken by a Troll-iling—a storm said to be raised by and to conceal a Troll—before which sticks and straws danced in the air. Quickly grasping his knife he threw it at the wind, which at once subsided, and in a few seconds the usual quiet reigned.

Some time later he was again hunting, when he lost his way. After a long and wearisome wandering he reached a Lapp hut, where he found a woman stirring something in a kettle. When she had concluded her cooking, she invited the hunter to dine, and gave him the same knife to eat with that he had thrown at the storm

The following day he wished to return home, but could not possibly discover the course he should take, whereupon the Troll woman—for his hostess was none other—directed him to get into the Lapp sled, and attach to it a rope, in which he must tie three knots.

"Now, untie one knot at a time," said she, "and you will soon reach home."

The hunter untied one knot, as instructed, and away went the rope, dragging the sled after it into the air. After a time he untied another knot, and his speed was increased. Finally he untied the last knot, increasing the speed to such a rate that when the sled came to a standstill, as it did, suddenly, not long after, he concluded his journey, falling into his own yard with such force as to break his leg.

The Lapp Genesis

The Lapps, like other people, have their legends, and many of them the same, or nearly so, as are found among other nations. Others reflect more particularly the national characteristics of the Lapp folk. Thus, for instance, there is to be found among them a tradition of a general deluge, a universal catastrophe, whereof there still remains a dim reminiscence in the consciences of so many other primitive people.

Before the Lord destroyed mankind, so says the Lapp legend, there were people in Samelads (Lappland), but when the Flood came upon the earth every living creature perished except two, a brother and sister, whom God conducted to a high mountain—Passevare—"The Holy Mountain."

When the waters had subsided and the land was again dry, the brother and sister separated, going in opposite directions in search of others, if any might be left. After three years' fruitless search they met, and, recognizing each other, they once more went into the world, to meet again in three years, but, recognizing one another now, also, they parted a third time. When they met at the end of these three years neither knew the other, whereafter they lived together, and from them came the Lapps and Swedes.

Again, as to the distinct manners and customs of the Lapps and Swedes, they relate that at first both Lapps and Swedes were as one people and of the same parentage, but during a severe storm the one became frightened, and hurried under a board. From this came the Swedes, who live in houses. The other remained in the open air, and he became the progenitor of the Lapps, who, to this day, do not ask for a roof over their heads.

Herman Hofberg

The Giant's Bride

More than with anything else, the Lapp legends have to do with giants and the adventures of mankind with them. The giant is feared because of his great size and strength and his insatiable appetite for human flesh. His laziness, clumsiness, and that he is inferior to the man in intelligence are, however, often the cause of his overthrow.

It is, therefore, commonly an adventure wherein the giant has been outwitted by a Lapp man or woman that concludes the giant stories.

There was one time a giant who made love to a rich Lapp girl. Neither she nor her father were much inclined toward the match, but they did not dare do otherwise than appear to consent and at the same time thank the Giant for the high honor he would bestow upon them. The father, nevertheless, determined that the union should not take place, and consoled himself with the hope that when the time arrived some means of defeating the Giant's project would be presented. Meantime he was obliged to set the day when the Giant might come and claim his bride. Before the Giant's arrival the Lapp took a block of wood, about the size of his daughter, and clothing it in a gown, a new cap, silver belt, shoes and shoe band, he sat it up in a corner of the tent, with a close veil, such as is worn by Lapp brides, over the head.

When the Giant entered the tent he was much pleased to find the bride, as he supposed, in her best attire awaiting him, and at once asked his prospective father-in-law to go out with him and select the reindeer that should go with the bride as her dower. Meanwhile the daughter was concealed behind an adjacent hill with harnessed reindeer ready for flight. When the reindeer had been counted out the Giant proceeded to kill one of them for supper, while the Lapp slipped off into the woods, and, joining his daughter, they fled with all speed into the mountains.

The Giant, after dressing the reindeer, went into the tent to visit his sweetheart.

"Now, my little darling," said he, "put the kettle over the fire."

But no move in the corner.

"Oh, the little dear is bashful, I'll have to do it myself," said he.

After the pot had been boiling awhile he again addressed the object in the corner:

"Now my girl, you may cleave the marrow bone," but still no response.

"My little one is bashful, then I must do it myself," thought he.

When the meat was cooked he tried again:

"Come, now, my dear, and prepare the meat." But the bride was as bashful as before, and did not stir.

"Gracious! How bashful she is. I must do it myself," repeated the Giant.

When he had prepared the meal he bade her come and eat, but without effect. The bride remained motionless in her corner.

"The more for me, then," thought he, and sat himself to the repast with a good appetite. When he had eaten, he bade his bride prepare the bed.

"Ah, my love, are you so bashful? I must then do it myself," said the simple Giant.

"Go now and retire." No, she had not yet overcome her bashfulness, whereupon the Giant became angry and grasped the object with great force.

Discovering how the Lapp had deceived him, and that he had only a block of wood instead of a human of flesh and blood, he was beside himself with rage, and started in hot pursuit after the Lapp. The latter, however, had so much the start that the Giant could not overtake him. At the same time it was snowing, which caused the Giant to lose his way in the mountains. Finally he began to suffer from the cold. The moon coming up, he thought it a fire built by the Lapp, and at once set out on a swift run toward it, but he had already run so far that he was completely exhausted. He then climbed to the top of a pine, thinking thereby to get near enough to the fire to warm himself, but he froze to death instead, and thus ends the story.

Herman Hofberg

The Cunning Lapp

A poor Lapp once ran into the hands of a Giant, by whom he knew he would be devoured if he could not conceive some means of outwitting him. To this end he therefore proposed that they have a contest of strength, the test to be that they should butt against a tree and see which could drive his head farthest into it. He who could make the deepest impression must, of course, be the stronger.

The Giant was first to make the trial. Taking his stand some distance from a tall pine, with a spring forward he drove his head with furious force against the trunk, but the most careful search did not discover a mark caused by the blow. The Lapp then said that he would show his strength the next day. During the night he

Swedish Fairy Tales

made a large hollow in the trunks of several trees and re-covered the cavities nicely with the bark. Next morning, when the contest was renewed, the Lapp ran from tree to tree, into each of which he thrust his head to his ears. The Giant looked on, thoroughly crestfallen at the exhibition of strength, but proposed that they have another trial. This time he who could throw an ice ax highest into the air should be declared the victor. The Giant threw first, and to such a height that the ax was almost lost to sight.

"That was a miserable throw," said the Lapp. "When I throw it shall be so high that it will lodge upon a cloud."

"No, my dear!" shouted the Giant. "Rather let me acknowledge myself the weaker, than lose my splendid ax." Thus again the Lapp came off champion.

The next day, as the Lapp and the Giant were out in company, the Lapp gathered a number of willow twigs and began twisting them together.

"What are you about to do with those?" asked the Giant.

"I mean to carry away your treasure house," answered the Lapp.

"Oh, my son," sighed the Giant, "let me retain my house, and I will fill your hat with silver."

"Very well," replied the Lapp.

While the Giant was away after the silver, the Lapp dug a pit, cut a hole in his hat crown and sat the hat over the pit.

"It's a big hat you have," complained the Giant.

"Fill it up!" shouted the Lapp. "Otherwise I'll throw you, as I would have done the ice ax, up into the clouds." And the Giant was compelled to give the Lapp such a sum of money that he was ever after a rich man.

Herman Hofberg

Kadnihaks

Kadnihaks are a kind of spirit which dwell underground, at times showing themselves to man dressed in red attire, and having long hair which resembles green flax and reaches to their waists. Like the Lapps, they have reindeer and clogs, and like them also in this and their dress, their language and songs are the same. Some of their songs have even been learned and are called "Kadniha-vuolle."

It happened in the last century that a great number of the mountain Lapps had pitched their tents in the vicinity of Qvikkjokk. It was at the season when the court and fair were in session in Jokkmokk. In the absence of the older people, in attendance at court or fair, the youths and maids remaining at home let themselves out for a good time at all kinds of games. An old Lapp woman, knowing that the Kadnihaks, or Trolls, living in the adjacent mountains would not tolerate such a confusion, warned the young people, but in vain.

Evening came, and all retired to rest, but it had hardly become quiet in the Lapp tents before the Kadnihaks were heard to be astir. The tinkling of bells, cries of men, barking of dogs, noise of reindeer and a general commotion prevailed on all sides.

The Lapps were seized with fear and trembling.

The old Lapp woman arose from her bed of reindeer skins and peeked out through the tent door. With horror she saw the whole tribe of sprites marching straight down upon the camp. No time was to be wasted. She threw about her a skin and hurried out to treat with the angry Trolls. With great trouble and promises that she would see to it that the children would conduct themselves better in the future, she induced them to change their course, thus staying the danger the camp was in of being trampled down. From that day there was quiet in the camp as long as it continued there.

Swedish Fairy Tales

Nu är sagan all.
Now the fairytale is over
(the fun is over).

—*Swedish Proverb*

Herman Hofberg

CPSIA information can be obtained
at www.ICGtesting.com
Printed in the USA
BVOW06s2224110218
507856BV00001B/12/P